SUGAR OBSESSION

SUGAR DADDIES #9

CHARITY PARKERSON

--Warning: This book is intended for readers over the age of 18.

Copyright © 2019 Charity Parkerson
Editor: BZ Hercules & Consultants
ISBN: 978-1-946099-45-7
All rights reserved.

INTRODUCTION

It was one innocent date that led to a single kiss. Infatuation was born.

When Tyrone and David agreed to attend John and Jonah's wedding together, that was all they meant the date to be. Tyrone doesn't have much room in his life for a man. He's more than a little surprised how drawn he is to David. Not only do they have a lot in common for two people who are several years apart in age and social status, there's a heat between them he can't deny. Still, Tyrone isn't sure that's enough to bridge the gap between them.

David has never been an overly emotional person. In fact, he's been single more years than he can count. Yet, he felt nothing lacking. Until Tyrone's kiss, that is. From the first skipped heartbeat in Tyrone's arms, nothing else matters. David needs all the messy emotions and entanglements he's avoided. He wants them with Tyrone and he won't stop until he wins. Unless Tyrone ends up dead first.

If David hopes to keep the man he loves safe, he must do things no one else would ever suspect. Tyrone is worth any risk.

ONE

HE COULDN'T SKIP THIS WEDDING. THAT WAS the mantra that kept Tyrone's foot on the gas pedal. Four months ago, Jonah Young had blown into Tyrone's life. He'd shown up late one night at Tyrone's emergency vet clinic with his dog in distress. Unfortunately, there'd been nothing Tyrone could do to save Jonah's pet, but he'd made a friend that night. At first, Tyrone only hoped to soothe Jonah's pain. Then, Jonah started volunteering at Tyrone's clinic. Day by day, they'd grown closer. Now, Jonah was set to marry the love of his life, John. Tyrone couldn't skip this one.

In a rare move, Tyrone had closed the clinic for the day, giving everyone the day off and the chance to attend Jonah's wedding. He'd posted a note on the door, giving directions to the closest animal ER. Hopefully, no one would be forced to use them.

In truth, it wasn't the wedding or the loss of business that truly had Tyrone on edge. It was his date for the wedding. At the thought alone, Tyrone's foot lifted, and his car slowed. He was so fucking out of his league and depth, Tyrone didn't know where to start. David Baker was one of those names. Everyone immediately recognized it. Whether they'd been to one of his many restaurants or had given money to one of his endless charities, everyone had heard the name. Then, Tyrone had met the man.

Tyrone sucked in a breath. At the time of their introduction, Tyrone made himself proud by keeping a cool head. It hadn't been easy. He'd been having lunch with Jonah and John, when David had appeared at the edge of their table. At Jonah's invitation, David had joined them. He'd slid into the booth next to Tyrone. They'd been inches apart. Tyrone had been transfixed. The man's name was household. In real life, David was stunning. It was impossible to guess his age by looking at him. David was the typical California elite. His light blond hair was graying at the temples. There were fine laugh lines around his unique blue eyes, but endless money made putting an actual age to his features impossible.

He could be forty, sixty, or anything in between. One thing was certain, though. David Baker was breathtaking. His sweet scent alone had Tyrone trying to shift subtly closer. Then John had suggested they attend the wedding together. At first, Tyrone had been slightly embarrassed. He didn't like looking hard-up for a date. But David's reaction changed everything. He'd seemed almost sad. It couldn't have been more obvious that he'd believed Tyrone wouldn't be willing to go with him due to their obvious age difference. Without another thought, Tyrone had found himself offering to escort David. Now the day was upon him and Tyrone was scared out of his goddamn mind. He was nervous and intimidated. Never before in his life had he been surer that he wasn't worthy.

The feeling of inferiority quadrupled as Tyrone came to the gate of David's property. As much as he'd known David owned a vineyard and farmland in addition to his countless restaurants, he realized too late he hadn't known a damn thing. This place was beyond anything Tyrone could've dreamed. The land went as far as the eye could see. Tyrone drove for several minutes down the driveway before spotting the house. Once he did, Tyrone couldn't believe his eyes. The place was massive and sprawling. There were stables beyond the house almost as large. His chest felt heavy—like he couldn't breathe from not belonging. Tyrone lived in a small home close to his office. Nothing about him or his lifestyle matched this place. Still, Tyrone parked in front of the brick stairs that led to the home's huge double front doors. He breathed through his nose, hoping to calm his nerves as he headed for the door. Before he had time to question if anyone would hear him if he knocked, the doors swung wide. An older lady with short gray curls and a bright smile greeted him.

"Welcome, Dr. Perry. David is still at the stables. Would you like to wait here or meet him down there?"

Tyrone paused. It seemed he'd been expected. As friendly as the woman seemed, Tyrone wasn't sure he wanted to linger in the foyer with her watching him and finding him lacking. "Um, the stables, I guess."

She nodded, seeming pleased with his choice. "Since you're looking spiffy for the wedding, I'd suggest you drive. Just follow the driveway and turn left at the entrance. You won't have any trouble finding David."

Tyrone gave her a sharp nod. "Thank you. It was nice meeting you..."

"Simone," she supplied.

"Simone," he repeated. "Have a great day."

"You too, Dr. Perry. I'm sure it'll be a beautiful wedding."

With a final wave, Tyrone headed back for his car. He imagined the wedding would be amazing. From Jonah's daily stories about the planning, Tyrone gathered it had been a struggle for Jonah to keep John's extravagance under control. Tyrone thought it was cute. Anyone could see how John worshipped the ground Jonah walked on. They gave him hope.

Following Simone's instructions made finding David easy. The second he stepped inside the stables, Tyrone had to force his feet to keep moving. David almost struck him immobile with his beauty. His tux looked incredibly out of place inside the horse barn. The embroidered jacket he wore had one button and molded to the man's sleek muscles. He was slim and tight. Expensive and unapproachable. Until he turned and met Tyrone's gaze, that is. David's eyes lit up with happiness. Tyrone couldn't even blink. He couldn't remember anyone ever looking at him the way David did—like seeing Tyrone made his day brighter.

"Wow." Tyrone couldn't stop the exclamation. He motioned David's way. "You look amazing. I feel like everyone will be wondering why you're with me."

David's mouth lifted in one corner, as if he fought the urge to call Tyrone a liar. "I had to break out my best for this one. Jonah came by last night, looking wrecked. He asked me to walk him down the aisle and I couldn't say no."

Tyrone nodded as he came to stand at David's side. "I'm not surprised. His father died when he was three and his mom has since disowned him. I should've suspected this wedding would bring all that to the surface."

David's gaze slipped down Tyrone's body. "You're wrong, by the way," he said as his gaze met Tyrone's again. "Everyone will be so busy looking at you, they won't have time for me."

Out of nowhere, Tyrone's cheeks heated. It was David's tone. The man wasn't simply returning Tyrone's compliment. He meant it. Tyrone tossed a glance around, searching for a way to turn the conversation elsewhere. His gaze landed on the stalls. There were several horses. He motioned toward them. "Were you on a final check before we leave?"

The way David visibly fought a smile made Tyrone wonder if he knew Tyrone was desperate to turn the topic from him. He nodded toward the horse closest to them. "Macy has been sick. She's getting on in years. I wanted to spend some time with her before we left. I lost track of the time." He blushed as he made the admission.

Tyrone felt a shift in his chest. Sometimes people looked at him like he was pathetic for loving animals more than humans most of the time. It couldn't have been more obvious David expected the same. Tyrone focused on the elderly horse to hide his reaction. "How old is Macy?"

"Thirty-three. I delivered her myself."

Tyrone gave Macy a pat. "Wow. You have lived a life, Macy. We're the same age." David made a sound close to choking behind him. Tyrone glanced over his shoulder. "Are you okay?"

A soft chuckle caressed Tyrone's ears. David's smile was unbelievably sexy. "Yes. Even though I realized you're younger than me, it's a bit of a shock actually hearing it."

"Now I have to know," Tyrone said with a laugh.

David's eyebrows rose, as if challenging Tyrone.

Tyrone held his gaze, waiting. David sighed. "I'm fifty."

Without thought, Tyrone gaze slid down David's gorgeous body before slowly moving back to hold David's stare. "I call bullshit."

A smile touched David's lips as the man shook his head. "You're a blatant flatterer, I see."

Tyrone shook his head. His gaze never wavered from David's amazing blue eyes. Each time he saw the man, Tyrone was floored anew by how unique they were. "I'm tragically honest."

A sexy chuckle fell from David's full lips. "Tragically?"

"To the point of hurting people's feelings, usually."

Silence and heat grew between them as they watched each other as if they each assessed the other's intentions. Tyrone shifted a step closer. Even he didn't know what he'd do next. A stall door opened feet away, surprising Tyrone enough he looked away. He hadn't realized they weren't alone. A dark-skinned man in a white t-shirt that stretched across his massive chest and arms and a straw cowboy hat stepped out. He was close to forty, Tyrone surmised in one glance before immediately returning to stare at David.

David's mouth lifted in one corner, as if he'd come to some conclusion he kept for himself. "Tyrone, this is Lawson Yates. He's in charge of basically everything and everyone around here except for me." Tyrone tore his gaze away from David to hold his hand out for Lawson as David continued the introduction. "Lawson, this is Tyrone Perry."

Lawson hesitated and wiped his hand on his jeans before accepting Tyrone's handshake. "It's nice to meet you. Do you go by Tyrone?"

"Most of the time, but my family and friends call me Ty."

"I figured as much," Lawson said with a grin. "I used to have a cousin named Tyrone and I don't think I've ever heard him called that. You can call me Law. Everyone does. You both look nice and ready for this wedding." Before Tyrone could respond, Lawson focused on David. "I don't imagine it'll be much longer. Maybe a day or two. Do you want me to call Dr. Estes?"

David stared at nothing, as if thinking things over before his gaze slid Tyrone's way. "What do you think, Dr. Perry? Is she suffering?"

He felt Lawson's stare but ignored the man in lieu of comforting David. Tyrone gave Macy a quick once over. She was old and obviously not much longer for the world, but she didn't seem to be struggling. "I think she's tired and will probably pass quietly. It's really more about how you feel at this point. You could have someone come out and give her something to keep her calm, keep her comfortable. I have a medical bag in my trunk if you'd like me to help out?"

David shook his head. "Law can call Dr. Estes. There's no sense in you risking your outfit. Plus," he paused and glanced at his watch, "we should probably be on our way."

He almost hated to leave now. It never took much to make him prefer being with animals, especially when needed, but they couldn't be late. David was walking Jonah down the aisle. That was huge. "You're right. Jonah might start panicking if you're not there soon." He glanced Law's way once more. "It was nice meeting you."

Lawson openly eyed him as if intrigued. "You too. Have fun and please pass along my felicitations."

"We will," David said, motioning Tyrone toward the door.

Tyrone fought the urge to glance over his shoulder as he led the way to his car. At the passenger side of his Lincoln MKZ, Tyrone opened the door for David. Their gazes met as David slid inside. Tyrone took a breath. He didn't know what it was about the man. As David had pointed out, there was a big difference in age, which was new for him. Normally, if Tyrone dated at all, he chose men younger than him. David also had a reserved strength about him. He didn't fill the world with unnecessary noise. Everyone Tyrone had been attracted to in the past were mostly sweet and chipper. Tyrone couldn't explain this date. David filled him with a possessive hunger Tyrone hadn't experienced before. He made it hard for Tyrone to catch his breath.

EVERYTHING ABOUT JOHN and Jonah's wedding turned out to be amazing, much to David's surprise. It wasn't that he thought the ceremony would be a disaster. David simply didn't enjoy weddings. Jonah looked adorable in his white tuxedo. He hadn't been nervous at all. In truth, David had shown more nerves than Jonah. Jonah walked down the aisle, proud to be heading toward John. John looked even larger than life in his black tux and air of expectancy. David worried the man would come bounding down the aisle and snatch Jonah from his feet in his obvious impatience. They made David wish for a life he'd never wanted. The entire day passed in a rushed blur. Everything from the kiss, the cake, and the dancing flew past with a sense of unreality. Everything except each time Tyrone touched him. David recalled each brush of skin with exact clarity. The way Tyrone draped his arm across the back of the pew behind David, tucking him close to his side during the ceremony, still warmed his skin. A small smile tugged at the corners of his mouth as he thought about the way Tyrone's hand found his beneath the table at dinner. When the music started, David found himself on his feet and in Tyrone's arms with no real thought as to how it happened. He'd given up two dances for Jonah, but every other song belonged to Tyrone. His chest felt unnaturally full.

Darkness surrounded them, only occasionally broken by a passing car's headlights brushing over Tyrone's features. David couldn't look away. Tyrone's muscular jaw and close-shaven hair kept him enthralled. There was something about the man currently driving him home. David wasn't a monk. He had people who kept him entertained, but he hadn't been serious about anyone in years.

Relationships took work. Work meant time. Time wasn't something David had much of to spare. David couldn't lie, though. He was interested, and Tyrone wasn't the type men played with. Even though he was considerably younger than David, Tyrone was a catch. He deserved someone with serious intentions. David didn't know if he was that person, but he couldn't deny the growing craving.

"I have a confession." The words were out there before David thought better of them. He was all in now. "I was dreading this wedding."

Tyrone looked away from the road long enough to cast David a look that screamed disbelief. "Really? Me too. Not because of you," Tyrone rushed to add.

"You either," David said, realizing how things sounded. "In general, I don't enjoy weddings, but this one." He shrugged, even though Tyrone wasn't looking at him. "I think this one made me a bit jealous." As the admission fell from David's lips, he wondered what it was about the dark that made confessions easier to spill.

"Me too." David heard the smile in Tyrone's voice. "I guess, before meeting Jonah, I didn't realize I was missing anything."

"Exactly," David agreed. They turned down David's driveway. He motioned at their surroundings. "I've always been content with running all this. Something about receiving John and Jonah's invitation left me deflated—like I've wasted my life. Sorry. It sounds pathetic now that I'm saying it aloud."

Tyrone parked at the front door and turned off the car. He met David's stare. "No. Don't apologize. I get what you're saying. For years, nothing has mattered more to me than my job. I'm passionate about it. More passionate than I've ever been about anyone I've ever met, and then Jonah came bursting into my life." A self-deprecating smile passed over Tyrone's face. "The way he lives for John and how John's world revolves around him, it makes me question my life choices." Tyrone glanced toward the house. "Let me walk you to the door."

Before David could argue he was capable of seeing himself inside, Tyrone slipped from the car and was at David's side, holding the car door open for him. David climbed out. He waited until after Tyrone closed the door so they could ascend the front steps side by side.

"I think you have a lot to be proud of," Tyrone said, sounding thoughtful. "You shouldn't be jealous of anyone. This place is amazing. In truth, I'm surprised by all this," Tyrone said, motioning toward their surroundings. "I don't know what I expected when I picked you up tonight. This mind-blowing place caught me off guard."

A small smile tugged at David's lips. "Honestly, sometimes it still surprises me."

Tyrone pulled a face, not bothering to hide his confusion. "How so?"

"I'm not my father," David answered. He knew that explained nothing to someone who never knew his father, but that was the truest answer he could give. At the front door, he faced Tyrone and tried to explain. "He was a farmer and a viticulturist. My dad believed in working the land and didn't care about much else. Of course, I was raised in two worlds. This," he said, motioning at their surroundings, "and California society. Even though I'd been taught hard work and earning my keep, my family still had money and I benefited from that. My mom passed away when I was young, so my father spoiled me more than he might have otherwise. While I went to the best schools and had the best of everything, I also couldn't unlearn the lessons I'd been taught here."

"You're a social activist." Tyrone smiled as he made the claim. David stared at the man's full lips. He made David forget his place.

"I suppose to some degree I am."

Tyrone nodded and looked around. "How did this turn into a chain of restaurants?"

David smiled. Even he heard the happiness in his voice. "As I said, I couldn't forget the lessons I'd been taught here. That doesn't mean I had any desire to be a farmer. I wanted to combine my two worlds, bringing organic and clean eating into the world of dining out and being on the go. With my family's money backing me, I struck out to carve a different path. I met people and realized I care about issues. One day, I was young and idealistic. It seemed like overnight, I was old and involved." David's smile fell. "Then my father passed, and overnight, all this was mine. I had to find a way to be everything he once was on top of my dreams." David shook head. "Sorry. I guess I'm..." He searched for the right term without luck.

"You're driven," Tyrone supplied. "I like it. My life has been the opposite of yours in many ways, but I'm the same. My parents were poor and struggled to provide even the basics for my brother and me. We understood there would be no money for college. In fact, we were lucky if there was food. I didn't want that life, so I studied harder than everyone I knew. Somehow, I landed a scholarship. Plus, I worked late hours and went hungry quite a bit, but I built my practice alone. It's everything. At least, it used to be." The last part of Tyrone's speech came out almost too low for David to hear. He wanted to ask, but then again, he didn't. David understood. This place had once been everything too. Lately, it felt like nothing because he was alone.

Rather than opening that wound, David chose a different track. "I imagine your parents must be extremely proud of all you've accomplished."

A sexy-sounding laugh fell from Tyrone's gorgeous lips and caressed David's ears. His smile and the laughter in Tyrone's eyes held David transfixed. "I remember how I used to picture my parents gushing with pride when I finally pulled off what no one else in my family ever had. But do you know what?"

David had to know. "What?"

"My brother is a goddamn astronaut." Laughter tinged each word Tyrone spoke. "That's the kind of shit you can't even make up. He works for the space program in Alabama."

The smile pulling at David's lips hurt his cheeks. Although he seemed to always wear a fake smile for society, David rarely smiled for real any longer. He hadn't stopped since meeting Tyrone. Even he didn't understand why. Tyrone was too young for him. They were both equally busy people. This was one date. "Would it be okay if I kiss you?" David didn't look away or blush as he made the request. He was too old to play games. If Tyrone said no, that would be the end of it. David couldn't end the night without trying.

Tyrone took a step closer. "I definitely think you should."

The backs of his knuckles skimmed the jawline that kept him fascinated in the car. His fingers found the back of Tyrone's neck. He urged the man closer. David held Tyrone's stare until the last second. He hadn't intended more than a brush of lips, but then their lips met. Tyrone shuffled even closer. The button on David's jacket loosened. Tyrone's palms slid across David's sides as Tyrone urged him even closer. David's lips parted as Tyrone urged him to open. The air thinned as their tongues met. They brushed. David lost himself. Tyrone kissed like he had all night. His tongue brushed David's before skirting away and licking the roof of David's mouth. A chuckle rose in David's throat. He recognized it was a game. Tyrone meant to tease him into chasing him. No one played with him. By nature, David was a serious person. But no one picked him up for dates either. In fact, he'd come to expect he'd always drive, pay, and lead. With one simple act, Tyrone had proven he wasn't like anyone else. He should've known Tyrone's kiss would be as unique as the man.

When he thought he'd adjusted to the playfulness, Tyrone changed tactics, deepening their kiss. David's blood boiled with lust. Tyrone's hands were never still, but his touch stayed respectful. David was the one fighting the urge to stroke Tyrone every place he could reach. Tyrone lightly nipped at David's bottom lip. For a moment, he held it there, sucking. When he leaned away, he looked ready for everything. His chest heaved as if he'd run for miles. He watched David through hooded eyes, looking ravenous.

"Thank you for going with me today. I hate to leave, but I should definitely go before it's too late."

David fought the urge to scream it was already too late and beg Tyrone to come inside. Instead, he nodded. "Thank you for today." His knuckles skimmed Tyrone's jaw again before his hand fell away. "This has been nicer than anything I can recall in a long while."

"Agreed," Tyrone said before pressing another quick kiss to David's lips and turning away. He jogged down the steps while David watched with longing in his heart. Even though he felt like a ridiculous teenager, David didn't move as Tyrone pulled away. He couldn't stop staring.

"Sorry to bother you, sir. It looks like Macy won't last the night."

At Law's sudden appearance behind him, David knew he'd been hanging out in the shadows awhile, waiting until David was alone. David glanced over his shoulder. "Let me change clothes, and I'll meet you at the stables."

"All right."

With a nod, David hurried inside and up the stairs to his bedroom. His body still burned with Tyrone's touch. David's lips stung with his kiss. Inside his bedroom, he quickly stripped away the expensive tux. As he opened the closet door, David caught sight of himself in the mirror. His eyes shone bright with lust and happiness. Without thought, his fingers moved to his lips. They were swollen. David almost didn't recognize himself. Somewhere along the way, he'd become immersed in business and forgotten to live. It was possible it was too late for him to find love. After all, tonight was only one date. Damn, what a date it had been.

David's hand slid lower, moving down his chest. He didn't look his age. Staying busy had kept him in decent shape. It wasn't too late. He wasn't ready to give up just yet. With a shake of his head, David grabbed some jeans and a t-shirt. It would be a long night. Maybe tomorrow, he'd toss everything to the wind and set out to seduce a sexy veterinarian. Who knew? He might win.

TYRONE HAD no idea how he made it home. He didn't remember a second of the drive. Each and every one of his thoughts were locked on that kiss. His mind was officially blown. He couldn't remember the last time he'd felt so desired. Tyrone doubted David was even conscious of the way he'd moved against Tyrone or the soft sounds he made—like Tyrone owned him in that moment. Jesus. Tyrone readjusted himself for the tenth time. He fought the urge to turn around. Not once had Tyrone begged for any man. Right now, he was tempted. He had a feeling David would be fucking amazing. Not once all day had Tyrone thought about work. Every brain cell he possessed had been focused on the next brush of skin. His next move. When he'd reached beneath the table at dinner and taken David's hand, he'd half expected the man to pull away. Instead, after a moment passed, David's thumb had brushed lightly back and forth across his. Tyrone took a deep breath. He couldn't accept this was only one date.

As Tyrone pulled into his driveway and his headlights swept across the porch, a loud groan filled the car. Coy sat on his front steps, leaned against the railing, waiting. No good could come of this. All lust disappeared. Coy was twenty-two and trouble. To Tyrone's shame, he'd slept with Coy more than a few times. It wasn't the difference in their ages that bothered him. Coy was the problem. He was blond haired and blue-eyed. Beautiful. Coy knew it too, and he used it to have his way. Tyrone always told himself that he had Coy's number. He wasn't getting used like everyone else, but every time Coy disappeared from his life, Tyrone realized he'd played himself. Coy had more fucking issues than a November ballot.

Tyrone didn't bother pulling into the garage. Coy's car wasn't there and he sure as fuck wasn't staying. Before Tyrone made it three feet away, he smelled the alcohol. Goddamn it. "What are you doing here, Coy?"

Coy smiled, using his gorgeous dimples against Tyrone the way he always did. "Hey, Ty. You don't sound happy to see me."

"Maybe if it was a decent time, or you were sober, I'd be happy. Better yet, maybe if you hadn't ghosted on me seven months ago, this visit wouldn't be so awkward."

"You're the one who works all the time," Coy argued, struggling to his feet. "You're the one who doesn't have time for me. I can't ghost on someone who's never around."

Tyrone bit back a growl. Same story. Different guy. Everyone wanted every second of his time or none. Except, he knew Coy too well. "What's his name?"

Coy hugged the rail and gave Tyrone his sexiest pout. "Do we have to do this? Can't you just be happy to have me here for once?"

Tyrone wanted to punch something. Coy always made him feel like the biggest bastard, but there was no other way to deal with him. "Come on. I'll drive you home."

A flash of hurt passed over Coy's features. "No. I'll walk." As he made the claim, he tripped down the stairs, forcing Tyrone to catch him. His perfect, compact body molded against Tyrone's. Their faces were inches apart. Coy's features softened in a move he'd perfected at way too young of an age. "I miss you, Ty," Coy whispered. "Am I that easy to forget?"

"If you cared about me at all, you'd be impossible to forget." Tyrone wasn't a liar. As much as he wanted to tell Coy he wasn't interested in the least, things would be different if Coy was.

"Of course I care about you." Coy sounded sad.

Tyrone wished his amazing night hadn't been ruined. He steered Coy toward the passenger side of the car and held his silence.

Coy didn't say another word until they were on the road. "You look nice," he said quietly. "I guess I don't fit in your life anymore."

While grinding his back teeth, Tyrone kept his gaze locked straight ahead. He took a breath. "I was at a wedding."

"Oh, that's nice. Anyone I know?"

"A volunteer at the clinic. You don't know him." Even Tyrone heard the disconnect in his voice.

"You smell nice too."

Tyrone took another breath. He smelled like David's expensive cologne. Damn. It had really been a great day. "What's got you plastered tonight? Don't say Crown. I can smell that much for myself."

"Just having an off night. Nothing big. Plus, I miss you a lot."

All that was bullshit, but whatever. Tyrone refused to dig into Coy's bullshit if the guy didn't want to invite him in. He nearly crowed in relief as Coy's apartment complex came into view. "Home. Safe and sound."

"Sure," Coy said, turning unreadable. "Safe and sound. Sorry for ruining your night." Coy jumped from the car without looking back the moment the car rolled to a stop. Tyrone fought the urge to bang his head on the steering wheel. For several minutes, he considered going after Coy. There was obviously something going on. In the end, he couldn't take the drama. David hadn't been dramatic all day. It had been... nice. Damn, he wished David had invited him inside. Tyrone could've avoided all this. Whatever happened next, Tyrone had to find a way to see David again. It mattered.

TWO

Tyrone stared at the enormous flower arrangement. Jonah was on his honeymoon. He was the only one who ever got flowers around there. Surely John wasn't still sending Jonah gifts while they were together and touring the world. Tyrone plucked the card from the vase and read.

Tyrone,

Thank you for escorting me to John and Jonah's wedding. You turned what I expected to be a depressing day for me into an amazing experience —David.

Tyrone went back to staring at the roses. They were for him. He didn't think he'd ever been sent flowers in his life. If he thought about it, though, David was the proper type. He was the kind of man who'd send a thank you gift. Still, Tyrone was speechless. David had expected the wedding to be a depressing day. Tyrone shook his head. Honestly, he'd expected the same. Instead, David had kept him fascinated. He wanted to call and thank David, but more than that, Tyrone wanted to see him. He dug his phone from the pocket of his lab coat and found David's number.

Tyrone: *I know—like me—you're always extremely busy, but is there a chance you'd be willing to have lunch with me? No pressure. I'll buy.*

He didn't expect to hear back right away and was more than a little surprised when his phone immediately buzzed with an incoming message.

David: *I'm visiting a few of my locations today. How about I grab something from one of my restaurants for us and bring it to you? That way, you don't have to worry about getting called away.*

Okay. This guy was amazing. Too good to be true, in fact. History had shown the other shoe would drop any time. Until then, Tyrone kind of wanted to see where things went.

Tyrone: *Sounds good.* He hesitated before adding, *I can't wait.*

There. He didn't want to seem overly eager, but he was more interested than he wanted to admit.

Still, Tyrone fought the urge to chew his nails while he waited. Half an hour passed. Tyrone stayed close to his office so no one would see him pacing and he could see the front door. It swung wide. Tyrone's gaze shot that way. David backed inside while holding two bags away from his body, keeping their food safe. All thoughts of seeming too eager fled. He rushed through the waiting room to help.

"Hey."

David's head turned his way. His eyes lit. "Hey."

Tyrone fought back an inner sigh. "Let me help," he said, reaching for a bag.

David passed it his way. "Thanks."

"This way." Tyrone nodded toward the hallway where his office was located. He carefully kept his gaze averted from the girl who worked the front desk. He could feel Kelly's knowing stare. She'd already seen him with David at the wedding. This was date two. She'd want to know more later. For now, he led David inside his office and closed the door before setting the bag on his desk. His gaze slid David's way. The top two buttons on his shirt were undone and his sleeves were rolled up to his elbows. Tyrone hadn't realized before that moment a man's neck and forearms could be so damn sexy. While David set his bag on Tyrone's desk, something inside Tyrone gave way. He closed the distance between them. His palm collided with David's hip as he crowded the man's space and peered over the man's shoulder.

"Smells good. What did you bring?" In truth, David's cologne was the only scent filling Tyrone's nose.

David turned his head. Their faces were only inches apart. Tyrone was struck dumb by the blue of David's eyes. David's gaze dropped to Tyrone's mouth. It was if all sense of reason and reality slipped away. In a flash of motion, he had David turned in his arms. Tyrone's body molded to David's. His lips found David's while his hands filled with David's ass. He squeezed even as he tried hauling David closer. Tyrone's teeth sank into David's bottom lip. David's gasp gave Tyrone exactly what he sought—access to David's tongue. Tyrone shoved his way inside and kissed David deep. His thin scrubs were no protection when he felt David go hard. Tyrone shifted forward, pinning David against the edge of the desk. He lifted, setting David on the desk and moving between the man's thighs. Tyrone had to taste the bare skin above David's collar. David dutifully tilted his chin up, giving Tyrone better access to his throat as Tyrone trailed kisses down his neck. His fingers dug into Tyrone's shoulders when

Tyrone nipped at his throat. Even Tyrone recognized he needed to calm down. He softened his kiss. His lips barely skimmed David's skin as he made his way back to David's lips. He hadn't meant for things to turn heated. Something about leaving unsatisfied last night and touching David now had exploded inside him.

"I'm sorry," Tyrone whispered against David's lips. He pulled back an inch. "I don't know what happened."

"Don't stop."

That was all the permission Tyrone needed to reclaim David's mouth. David kissed him back every bit as desperately. That was why he couldn't stop. Tyrone hadn't felt such a strong connection with anyone in a long time. He more than liked David. Tyrone could see himself with him.

A soft knock landed on his door, causing a growl to rise in his throat. He let David's feet slip to the floor. The last thing he wanted was to embarrass David.

"What?" Even Tyrone heard the growl in his voice.

Kelly sounded apologetic as she spoke through the door. "You have a visitor."

David wandered over to the bookshelf and eyed

Tyrone's pictures and degrees. Tyrone wondered if he needed a minute to get his body under control like Tyrone did. He adjusted his lab coat, doing his best to hide his erection before throwing open the door. Coy slipped inside the room without waiting for an invite. He looked exactly like someone who'd been drunk off his ass only hours earlier. His blonde hair was a strategic hot mess, and he had a bruise in the corner of his eye Tyrone hadn't noticed last night.

"I came to apologize about last night."

Tyrone looked David's way without thought. He couldn't let David think anything happened with Coy. They weren't a couple, but no one appreciated being left at the door by someone who moved on to someone else's bed. "There's nothing to apologize for."

If Coy noticed they weren't alone, he didn't let on. "I shouldn't have turned up on your doorstep drunk. You deserve to have me sober."

Tyrone refused to play this game. He focused on David, who was now silently watching their every move. "I took him straight home and left him at his front door unmolested."

David's mouth lifted in one corner, as if he found Tyrone's current predicament humorous. "No need to explain."

Coy glanced between them as if finally catching on. "I didn't realize." Tyrone's eyebrows rose, challenging Coy to finish that statement. Instead, Coy's expression snapped closed. He gave Tyrone a sharp nod and shoved his hands in his pockets. "That's all. I just wanted to say I'm sorry. Thanks for the ride. I'll get out of your way." His gaze slid David's way once more before he quickly dipped out the door.

As he closed the door behind Coy, Tyrone ran his hand over his face. There was nothing quite like an ex showing up to ruin the mood. "Jesus. I'm sorry." Tyrone turned to find his back against the door and David's mouth finding his. It seemed he wasn't upset about the intrusion.

"What are you doing tonight?" David asked as he pulled away.

Tyrone blinked, trying to make his mind work properly. "Um. After eight, I'm on call, but barring any emergencies, I'm free."

"Good," David said, pushing away. "Come see me." He headed toward the desk as if things were settled.

Tyrone couldn't look away from the man's sexy ass. "Okay." He was there. Whatever David wanted. Tyrone was so fucking there.

AFTER TYRONE MOVED past his obvious horror over having his young stalker appear, they had a nice lunch. David fought the urge to laugh every time he thought about Tyrone's expression as the blond kid had burst into the room. Little did Tyrone know, David wasn't so easily budged. He had his sights set on Tyrone. David always got what he wanted.

It was harder than expected to leave. If Tyrone didn't have appointments, David might've sat down and refused to move. Damn, he hadn't wanted anyone as badly in a long time. Several times, he opened Tyrone's office door an inch, only to have Tyrone push it closed again to reclaim his mouth. He was taking their leftovers with him only so he had something to hide his erection on the way out.

"You have appointments," David reminded him as Tyrone's lips skimmed his throat.

With a loud sigh, Tyrone backed away. "Sometimes being a responsible adult sucks."

David nodded. He couldn't agree more. "Tonight. After eight."

"Am I taking you away from anything?"

Nothing David wanted more than Tyrone.

"Don't worry over my schedule. Just see me when you can."

"Okay. I'll be there."

David nodded and slipped away on Tyrone's promise. He almost felt a little ridiculous about how giddy he was, but the embarrassment wouldn't take hold. David was too excited. Everything about Tyrone was amazing. David tossed their trash in the dumpster and headed for his Bentley.

"I figured that must be your car."

David turned to find the blond guy from earlier leaning against the side of the building, as if he'd been waiting for David. "I'm not sure why you'd think of me at all, but you're correct."

"I'm Coy."

David dipped his chin. He didn't offer his name because he wasn't sure Coy was the boy's name. It was possible he was just irritatingly honest.

When David didn't respond, the boy's face hardened. "He won't choose you over me. You get that, right?"

A slow smile spread across David's lips. No one had challenged him in a long time. A chuckle that sounded evil even to his ears escaped David. "Pathetic and desperate isn't the new sexy, but that's cute." Another laugh escaped him. He couldn't help it. It wasn't confidence driving David. There was a real possibility Tyrone would choose youth and obvious free time over David. In truth, Tyrone would probably be better off with this man child. The guy's posturing, though, that was hilarious. David shook his head. "Ah, to be young," he said under his breath as he slipped inside his car. Everyone should get to be so stupid at least once.

David's humor over the situation lasted the rest of the day. By ten, it was gone. Tyrone wasn't there yet, and he hadn't called. David didn't know whether he should call or keep waiting. Even though he didn't want to suspect the worst, there was still a tiny voice whispering he might be wrong. Maybe young, attractive stalkers were what turned Tyrone's head. By eleven, he was done. He wasn't a worrier by nature and he knew his worth. David would go to bed and forget it. His phone chirped. The way David jumped for it screamed he was a liar. He was desperate for Tyrone.

Tyrone: *I'm so sorry. It's been back-to-back emergency visits all night. I've been putting off texting you, hoping against hope I could still make it. Normally, I never text anyone past ten, but I couldn't let you think I'd forgotten you. It doesn't look like it'll happen, and I don't want you waiting all night. Let me know when I can make it up to you and I'll do my best.*

David: *Don't worry over it at all. I knew you were on call. We'll figure something out when you have more time.*

There. He'd managed to not sound desperate at all. David fought the urge to pat himself on the back. Now he just had to make it through another lonely night. Damn. He was tired of living like this. Funny how he hadn't noticed until Tyrone. Now his bed felt colder than ever.

THREE

THE ROADS WERE DEAD AT FIVE IN THE MORNING. It was a good thing, since David hadn't slept all night and wasn't in the mood to deal with traffic. Tyrone hadn't texted him again. David had a bad feeling he knew why and now he was the stalker. He told himself he wouldn't stop. David just needed to know if Tyrone was okay. Yeah, he knew how it looked, but no one would ever know he'd climbed in his car and driven to Tyrone's office, because David planned to take it to the grave. Even he couldn't explain his actions. There was a bad feeling in the pit of his stomach. He needed to know if it was due to a blond stalker or if Tyrone was dead in a ditch. His gut feelings always led him right, even if he didn't know why sometimes. When he reached the clinic,

Tyrone's car was parked in the same spot as it had been the day before. It didn't look like it had moved at all. At the stop sign, David chewed his bottom lip. Fuck it. He pulled in and parked next to Tyrone. If he looked crazy, then he did. As he cleared the front door, the same blonde who'd worked the day before sat behind the desk. She smiled as she caught sight of him.

His gaze dropped to her name tag. "Good morning, Kelly."

Her smile brightened. "Good morning. Dr. Perry is in his office. You can go on back."

He nodded his thanks and headed for Tyrone's office. The door stood open. David spotted Tyrone, head on desk and sleeping, before he cleared the door. One half of his scrubs were crusted with blood. David's heart squeezed in his chest at the sight. It was obvious Tyrone had a long and hard night. David crossed the room. His hand slid across Tyrone's back before he could stop himself. He needed to comfort Tyrone. It was out of his control. Tyrone's head shot up. He blinked, looking lost. His gaze landed on David and his face softened. "Hey." His shoulders fell. "I ruined our date."

David wanted to kiss him. His lips tingled with

the desire. "Come on. Let me take you home. You shouldn't be driving like this."

Tyrone looked around and then glanced at his watch. "I can't go home. I have appointments."

They obviously hadn't met. Otherwise, Tyrone would know David wasn't someone to be disobeyed. He headed back to the door and poked his head out. "Hey, Kelly."

She appeared at his call. "Yes?"

"Is there anyone you can call to cover for Tyrone, so he can go home and get some sleep?"

She nodded. "Yes, sir."

"Let's do that."

"Yes, sir."

He flashed her a grateful smile and went back to retrieve Tyrone. "There. Your appointments are covered. Let's go."

Tyrone shook his head. "You know she works for me, right? I just need some fresh scrubs and I'll be good."

David waited until he'd muscled Tyrone toward the front door before putting his foot down. "Not to sound like a dick, but it seems to me you need someone to tell you no and when to stop. It's time to stop. You need sleep. Now let's get in the damn car."

"Thank you," Kelly mouthed over Tyrone's shoulder.

David nodded, doing his best to reassure her. It was obvious Tyrone's staff cared about him "I've got him." As David helped Tyrone into the passenger side of his car, he realized he had no clue where he was going. He'd take Tyrone to his house, but then the guy wouldn't have any clothes. "What's your address?"

Tyrone leaned his head back and closed his eyes as David snapped his seat belt in place. "1908 Poplar Lane."

GPS would get David there. He wasn't worried about getting directions. Halfway to his destination, David's ire grew. He'd worked himself into the ground more years than he could count, but this was nuts. "When was the last time you ate?"

"With you," Tyrone answered, proving he was still awake despite his closed eyes.

David swallowed a growl. "When was the last time you slept a full eight hours?"

"Two thousand and ten."

A snort escaped David. "You're a complete mess."

"I stink too. You shouldn't have put me in your car without stripping me."

The heat in Tyrone's voice had David's smile growing in spite of his anger. "Don't worry about my car. I'll strip you when we get home. You need a shower."

Tyrone released a jaw-cracking yawn while trying to talk around it. "Do you plan to join me?"

David's eye roll was out of his control. "No."

"So you are mad at me."

"No. I don't take advantage of weakened men."

"I'm sorry our plans got ruined."

David bit back a sigh. "Please stop apologizing. I'm not some needy teenager who sits at home, pining and pacing. You have a job that comes before me. I'll survive it."

"Huh," Tyrone said, sounding taken aback. "That's the first time anyone accused me of putting my job above them that it felt untrue. I didn't want to be at the office last night. In fact, at one point, I was downright resentful, but I couldn't leave. I wanted to be with you."

Each word Tyrone spoke came out sounding less awake than the last. Still, even David's heart smiled. He didn't need Tyrone to put him above his job. Yet his insides warmed at the idea. They still weren't officially a couple. He shouldn't want or expect anything. But they felt like a real couple. David wanted to be with Tyrone more than he wanted to do anything else. That was rare for him.

"I'll take care of everything," David said quietly, in case Tyrone had fallen asleep. He didn't say another word throughout the drive, hoping Tyrone would sleep. When the GPS informed him they'd arrived at their destination, David turned into the driveway. The house was in a cul-de-sac. It was nice but surprisingly modest for a doctor. Red brick and probably no more than four bedrooms, the house looked like a place a family would live. Hell, it was probably a good school district. There was nothing wrong with the place. David just expected something else—like a small farm, which might seem odd to anyone else, but Tyrone loved animals. Yet, he was here without even a fenced-in backyard. It was... odd.

Tyrone climbed out, proving he was still awake and functioning. David followed on his heels to the front door. "Point me toward your kitchen and I'll find you something to eat while you shower."

"Ugh," Tyrone said, pushing through the door. "The idea of food makes me feel sick. Why don't you come with me instead? I might fall if left alone."

David bit the inside of his cheek to keep from smiling. Tyrone was still trying to get David in the shower with him, even though he was half dead. "I'll sit in the bathroom with you, but you can shower alone."

"Fair enough."

He should've known by Tyrone's too-agreeable tone that it wouldn't be that simple. Tyrone's shower door turned out to be crystal clear and Tyrone made sure David got a show. At first, while Tyrone stripped and stepped beneath the stream, he'd tried keeping his gaze averted. Tyrone kept forgetting things, forcing David to hand them to him, and making conversation, leaving David no choice but to look. It seemed wrong to ogle a man who could fall over asleep at any moment, but damn. Tyrone was beautiful. He had the perfect ass—round and firm. David's eyes kept sliding that way before he caught himself and looked away again. When the water turned off, David was there with a towel, poised to cover Tyrone before temptation hobbled him. While holding Tyrone's stare, he wrapped the towel around the man's waist.

Tyrone smirked, making David's mouth go dry. "It's like you think I'll judge you if you look."

"You're exhausted, so I'd judge me."

"I'm tired, but I'm not out of my head," Tyrone assured him. Tyrone shuffled closer. His hand rose.

David didn't back away. Tyrone's knuckles brushed David's cheek. He didn't stop there. Tyrone swiped his thumb along David's bottom lip. His eyes followed the move. "I like you," Tyrone whispered. His gaze lifted to David's. "A lot more than I've liked anyone in longer than I can remember."

David couldn't move. He was held captive by Tyrone's intensity. "I like you too."

"Is there an adult way of asking if we can date exclusively? Every way I think to phrase it sounds childish."

A smile tugged at David's lips. "I think you pulled it off with aplomb, and I'd like that."

"You probably had a great night's sleep, but will you come to bed with me?"

"To sleep?"

A sexy-sounding chuckle escaped Tyrone. It also sounded tired. "Yes. I'll behave."

"Then, yes." As Tyrone took his hand and led him toward his king-sized bed, David couldn't fight back a confession. "I didn't sleep at all last night or the night before that, since I was up with Macy until she passed."

"Oh, damn. I'm sorry. I didn't even think to ask about Macy. I'm not starting this thing out at my best." Tyrone flipped back the dark covers for David.

He climbed in. "As I've said, I know you're busy." As David settled in, Tyrone moved to the window and pulled down a blackout shade. It didn't completely plunge the room into darkness, but it helped. David's gaze followed Tyrone's every step as the towel fell away. He pulled on a pair of boxer briefs. David breathed through his nose. His control was tested like never before. As if Tyrone sensed his weakened state, he went straight for the button of David's jeans as he crawled beneath the covers. "There's no way you'll sleep in these clothes."

"There's no way I'll sleep out of them."

Tyrone's mouth lifted in one corner. "You'd be surprised. I'm one hell of a cuddler." He couldn't turn down such a confident boast. David let Tyrone have his pants. Tyrone wasn't content to stop there. He urged David out of his shirt as well. "I'm keeping this," Tyrone said, cramming the shirt beneath his pillow. "That way, you can't sneak away while I sleep."

A snort escaped David. "Seriously? I don't sneak."

"Good. I have plans for you later." The promise in Tyrone's voice as he hauled David into his arms had David fighting a huge grin. Damn, Tyrone was under his skin. "Of course, you can't sleep without kissing me first."

"You're so demanding. Sleep with me. Give me your clothes. Don't sneak away. Kiss me."

"If you insist," Tyrone said, rolling and tucking David beneath him. His mouth came down on David's. He wanted to stay detached for the sake of Tyrone needing his rest. The last thing he wanted was to curl up in Tyrone's arms, horny as hell, and try to nap. Every kiss from Tyrone was unique. This one had David's heart turning over in his chest. It was the sweetest brush of lips on lips followed by the lightest brushing of tongues. Tyrone's hand caressed his thigh, lifting it higher as he rocked against David. David sucked in a breath as he went hard. There was next to no clothing between them. He cared about Tyrone. The man needed to recharge. David didn't have the strength to stop.

"Tell me to go to sleep," Tyrone pleaded between kisses.

"Go to sleep."

A groan vibrated against David's lips, making his dick twitch. "Is that really what you want?" Tyrone massaged David's dick through his underwear as he asked the question.

David writhed against his touch. "I'm looking out for your health."

Tyrone's fingers curled around the edge of David's underwear, balling the material in his hand. He dragged it down David's hip. "I'm looking out for my mental health," he said, shifting onto his knees and stripping away the last articles of clothing standing in his way. His gaze skirted down David's nude body, openly eyeing every inch. David did the same while trying not to squirm. "Goddamn," Tyrone breathed before covering David's body with his once more and reclaiming his mouth.

David's fingers dug into Tyrone's back as he tried getting as close as possible. He couldn't stop sucking Tyrone's bottom lip. It was the perfect level of plumpness.

"I want you on my dick."

David lost his breath at Tyrone's claim. He loved a talker. He didn't want to try to guess what pleased someone in bed. Tyrone didn't hold back.

"I like this plan." At David's agreement, Tyrone dove for the table next to the bed. After finding the lube and a condom, Tyrone rolled onto his back and ripped open the gold packet. As David looked on, he rolled the sheath down his length while David's mouth watered. Even Tyrone's cock was sexy. Tyrone coated the outside of the condom with lube.

"Come here."

That was all the urging David needed to straddle Tyrone's body. Tyrone pulled him down for another kiss. With their tongues entwined, Tyrone fingered David's asshole, stretching him and using the lube to ease things. His crown pressed against the ring of muscles surrounding David's asshole. He pushed. David dropped his forehead to Tyrone's chest and gasped at the intrusion. His cock tapped Tyrone's stomach. A line of pre-cum dripped from David and clung to Tyrone's skin. Tyrone held him still, giving him time to adjust. He felt full, but he needed to move.

"Holy shit, David. You're so hot. You're trying to suck me deeper. I don't know if I'll last long."

With his hands braced against Tyrone's chest, David readjusted his position and rode Tyrone like a horse. Every sound Tyrone made drove David. Tyrone grabbed David's dick and tugged. David's eyes rolled back in his head at the move. Tyrone beat at David's dick at a pace David couldn't match. He could barely breathe. His hips lifted, seeking the release Tyrone's hand promised. Tyrone's dick massaged his insides, making him insane. There was no thought or skill in his moves. He was on autopilot, blindly chasing an orgasm.

"Tyrone. Damn. Please?"

"You're so beautiful," Tyrone praised. His rhythm never slowed. "Let me watch you come, sexy. I need to feel that ass when your body comes unglued."

Pressure climbed his shaft. David reached for release. Pleasure rocked him, stealing his breath. His gasp rang through the room as his cum coated Tyrone's dark skin.

Tyrone tilted his head back. With his mouth open in a silent scream, his fingers dug into David's skin as he ground against him, taking his pleasure from David's ass. A haze of ecstasy coated David's brain, but he couldn't look away as Tyrone's body stiffened. An animalistic grunt escaped Tyrone. He towed David down, squeezing him against his chest, uncaring of the mess.

"Oh my god," Tyrone gasped out between breaths. "It'll be better when I'm not so tired."

David's body shook with laughter. "Better? I'm not sure if my heart can take it."

Tyrone sounded like he struggled to breathe. "You'll get a lot more foreplay. I was just too desperate for you this time. Next time, you'll be impressed."

David shook harder. Happiness and exhaustion had him out of his head. "You might kill me if you impress me more."

"We'll go together with smiles on our faces."

David couldn't stop smiling now. He snuggled closer, needing to be in Tyrone's arms, no matter the cum squishing between them. One day, they'd be rested and have time on their hands. Until then, David had no complaints.

FOUR

An incessant buzzing drove David insane. His eyelids were too heavy to lift, while his body floated in the clouds. He couldn't recall the last time he'd been so comfortable he didn't want to move. The perfect pillow warming him shifted, dragging a groan of denial from him.

The sexiest rumble of laughter he'd ever heard vibrated against his ear. "Sorry, gorgeous. That's my emergency line."

David rolled away, freeing Tyrone. He pried his eyes open to enjoy the show of watching Tyrone's nude ass as he crossed the room to retrieve his phone.

"Dr. Perry."

David bit his lip to stop the hum of pleasure on

his tongue from escaping. Tyrone's voice was heavy with sleep and twice as sexy. He wanted Tyrone back in bed.

"Why would he... is he okay?"

David sat up as Tyrone's tone changed, becoming agitated and worried.

"Okay. Text me the information. I'll handle it when I can. Thanks, Kelly." Tyrone tossed the phone aside and climbed back in bed. He snagged David around the waist and hauled David against him as he settled in.

David snuggled as close as possible. "Is everything okay?"

Tyrone didn't answer right away. When he did, he sounded hesitant. "I'm not sure." He kissed the spot below David's ear before continuing. "It seems Coy put me down as his emergency contact, and he's in the hospital."

So the boy's name really was Coy. "Is he okay?"

He felt Tyrone shrug. "When the hospital couldn't get hold of me, they called the office. They couldn't release any info to Kelly."

David closed his eyes for a moment. Being an adult meant sometimes being the adult. "Come on. Get dressed and I'll take you over there."

Tyrone held him tighter, refusing to let David go. "It's Coy, so I'm sure it's not much more than a whole lot of drama. Plus, I don't leave a bed you're in to run to someone else's side."

David tried not to smile. He couldn't claim Tyrone wasn't making his preference known. "He's young." David left it at that. He didn't think it necessary to expound. Being young meant being dramatic and making mistakes. It also meant needing people to be there sometimes with a helping hand, even when the theatrics were at an all-time high.

Tyrone kissed his neck, sending goosebumps skirting across his skin. "You're too good for me."

"Don't make me out to be a saint. I'll disappoint you."

"I doubt it." Tyrone's words sounded muffled against David's skin as he trailed kisses down David's spine.

"I'm disappointing you now. It's time to get dressed so I can take you to the hospital."

Even though Tyrone grumbled, his concern showed itself in the way he rushed to dress. On the drive, Tyrone's knee bobbed, and he chewed on the side of his nail. He could pretend he didn't care, but David saw through the ruse. Tyrone wasn't the type to ignore suffering, whether it was an animal or an ex. David wasn't bothered. Tyrone's beautiful heart was one of things David liked about him.

At the hospital, a nurse in pink scrubs directed them to the third floor. David followed on Tyrone's heels. When they reached Coy's room, Tyrone tapped his knuckles on the door lightly.

"Come in."

Tyrone glanced David's way as he pushed open the door. He could practically hear Tyrone's thoughts screaming at him. Coy sounded fine.

Coy didn't look fine. David's eyebrows tried hitting his hairline at the first sight of Coy. His face was more bruises and dried blood than face. There were full handprint bruises around his arms in several places. Someone had done this to him.

"Jesus, Coy. What happened?"

Coy's gaze moved between Tyrone and David. He made no attempt to hide how betrayed he felt over David's presence. The emotion flashed in his eyes. "It's not a big deal. I only had the hospital call you because they said I couldn't leave unless someone signed a paper stating they would care for me for the next twenty-four hours. I don't expect that, of course. Since I don't have health insurance, I can't afford to keep staying here."

"I'm not signing shit until you tell me what's happened." Tyrone sounded half enraged and half concerned—like he didn't know which side he'd land on.

Coy's light blue eyes stood out even brighter while surrounded by bruises. His gaze moved between them again. He looked defeated as he dropped his chin and stared at his lap. Coy toyed with the white sheet covering his lap. "King happened," he finally said almost too quietly to hear.

"Who's King?" Tyrone's question proved he'd heard the man just fine.

"The guy I've been dating the past six months."

Tyrone sat—hard. He dropped into the closest chair as if his knees wouldn't hold him. "Some guy you've been dating did this. Is this the first time?"

Coy's shoulder lifted in a half shrug, but he still didn't look away from his lap. "It's the first time it was this bad." Coy's chest expanded on a deep breath. He finally lifted his chin and focused on Tyrone. "Look, Ty. I don't want anything from you. They won't let me leave here unless someone helps me. Just say that's you, and you're free to go. I'm not trying to pull you into my mess."

Tyrone shook his head. "Why didn't you call your mom?"

An ugly-sounding snort escaped Coy. "This is like her biggest fear coming true. You know I can't do that to her. From the moment she realized I'm gay, she's worried how society will treat me and how men will treat me. She supports me in every way, but she'll never sleep again if she sees me now. Seriously, Ty. You don't have to do anything for me. I just need out of here."

"And where will you go from here?" David asked, chiming in.

Coy visibly fought not to roll his eyes. David felt it in his soul. "I'm not homeless, or maybe I am, but I can go to a hotel."

"What's wrong with your apartment?" Tyrone asked before David could continue his questioning.

"King lives there too now."

"Jesus, Coy. You had me take you back there the other night, knowing this could happen."

"Do you have a job?" David asked, talking over Tyrone before Tyrone said something he couldn't take back. Being scared made people stupid.

"Not everyone is as blessed as you," Coy said. His rage was barely veiled. "Since I worked at King's bike shop, it looks like the unemployment line for me."

"Goddamn it," Tyrone cursed. "Why did you leave your job at the casino?"

David continued talking over Tyrone. "How do you plan to pay for a new place or to eat?"

"Seriously?" Coy said, sounding tired. "What's with all the questions?"

David shrugged. "I'm being realistic. If you don't have a job and can't pay to find a new place, then you can guarantee this guy will wait until you're at your lowest to weasel his way back into your life. He'll show up when you're on the edge of frustration, hungry, and dodging this hospital bill. Everything he says will sound better than the shit you're living in and you'll go back. It's in your eyes. You don't care about yourself anymore."

"David..."

David ignored Tyrone's half-assed attempt to intercede.

Coy's pretend patience vanished. His eyes flashed with hatred while locked on David. "No one asked you to come here to kick me while I'm down. Yes, I get it. Ty is yours and I'm inconveniencing you. You won. I lost. Well, get in fucking line. Other people got here first to mock me."

"Or I could give you a job and a place to stay so you don't have to even consider going back," David shot back. Coy had fire and David wasn't heartless. He sat on the board of a charity that ran a helpline for gay victims of domestic assault. There were many charities run by churches, although he'd learned over the years that a lot of religious organizations weren't willing to help the LGBT community. There was a need. He sought to fill it. Coy didn't strike David as having a victim mentality. He just needed help.

Coy visibly floundered for a full minute. "What?" he finally choked out. "Why would you, of all people, offer me a job? Is this some attempt to make me indebted to you?"

David shook his head. He tried his best to not be patronizing. That was not what Coy needed. "You obviously need someone in your corner and I'm in the position to do it. There's a job open at my place. It comes with room and board if you're interested. We can go straight there, and you can hang out until you're well enough to start work."

Coy balled the sheet in his fist. He looked ready to snap. "I'm not interested in being your lackey so you can put me in my place."

David fought a growl. Coy was the angriest person he'd ever met. "You wouldn't answer to me directly. You'd report to my property manager, Lawson. If you get started and hate it, you're free to leave at any time. At least let us try to give you an out from this King guy. This isn't pity or anything else you're picturing. I just want to help."

With his gaze locked on the wall, and the blanket still held tightly in his hand, Coy gave a sharp nod. David didn't feel even a hint of triumph at Coy's agreement. In fact, a hollow pit opened in David's gut, almost as if he'd signed the man's death warrant.

TYRONE'S MIND whirled a million miles a minute. He fought the urge to turn in his seat and pepper Coy with questions. The only thing stopping him was Coy's obvious fight to stay awake. It seemed they'd pumped him full of painkillers shortly before Tyrone's arrival. Tyrone couldn't recall a time he'd been more pissed. He was mad at Coy for getting himself into this position. He was angry with himself for driving Coy home the other night, delivering the man to god only knew what punishment. There'd been something in Coy's eyes and tone. Yet Tyrone had ignored all the warning bells because he wanted Coy out of his hair. Was it his fault? Coy had come to him, looking for an out. Had turning Coy away been the moment that sealed this fate? Tyrone couldn't stop. Logically, he recognized that it was Coy's choices and not his, but no one deserved this. If there was any chance he could've intervened, he owned some of the blame. Now David was the one stepping up like he should have. David...

Tyrone focused on David's profile as the man drove. He looked in control—like no racing thoughts owned him. His mind was set on helping, end of discussion. He was the most amazing person Tyrone had ever met. Tyrone didn't deserve him. This was a lot. David taking in Tyrone's ex, giving him a job and a safe place to stay; it was more than anyone could ask or expect. It was too much.

Tyrone glanced over his shoulder. Coy was out. His gaze found David's profile once more. Without thought, Tyrone's hand lifted. He brushed the shell of David's ear, tracing its shape with his thumb. A smile curved David's cheek. Tyrone couldn't stop touching him. He adored that smile. "You're beautiful," he said quietly, hoping not to disturb Coy. "Inside and out," he added, because he needed David to know he saw something in him. "I'm sorry my life exploded on you in the craziest of ways."

"It didn't, but you're worth it. You'll find I'm used to taking control of every situation. This was no different."

Tyrone's hand dropped to David's shoulder. From there, he brushed down David's arm before linking fingers with him. In silence, they held hands. Tyrone soaked up every second. The warmth of David's hand and the comfort in their silence had Tyrone's eyelids growing heavy. He still hadn't slept but a couple of short hours. His eyes slipped closed. David touched his arm and Tyrone's head shot up. He blinked in surprise at the sight of David's house.

"Come on. I'll get Coy settled and then you're going back to bed. Be prepared to surrender your phone first. I'm putting out the 'do not disturb' sign."

Tyrone was too tired to argue. He followed on David's heels, stopping when he stopped, barely aware of his surroundings.

Law appeared, as if waiting for instructions. David motioned Coy's way. "Law, this is Coy. Pick a room for him. Once he's well enough to work, you can assign him some duties. He'll need a few days of rest first."

Law eyed Coy. He didn't flinch as he took in the handprint bruises or cuts. His expression didn't show an ounce of judgment. He motioned for Coy to follow. "Come on. I'll find you a room on the first floor. You don't look ready to climb stairs yet."

Coy nodded and followed. He didn't glance

Tyrone's way. In fact, he kept his gaze locked on his toes. Tyrone's stomach muscles clenched at the defeat etching his every move. Despite Coy's earlier fire, he wasn't sure Coy would be okay. Maybe once Tyrone had some sleep, he'd know what to do. Right now, he kind of wanted to kill some guy named King who owned a bike shop, but he was smart enough to recognize that wouldn't solve anything. Possibly.

The moment they were alone, David gave Tyrone a pat down, stealing his phone and keys. He tossed them on a table near the foot of the stairs. With nothing left to disturb them, David led Tyrone up the stairs. By the time they made it to a set of large wooden doors, Tyrone was ready to curl up on the floor just to get some sleep. He wasn't sure how many steps he had left in him. David threw open the doors, revealing a cavernous room. A giant bed sat on a raised area in the center. It looked bigger than a king. Tyrone had never seen anything like it. Everything smelled like polished wood and David's cologne. He tried looking in every direction while David stripped him down to his underwear.

"Get in the bed."

Tyrone nodded and climbed the steps leading to the bed. He pulled back the deep maroon covers and climbed in. The ridiculously plush mattress swallowed him, beckoning him to become one with the bed. David's body molded against his. Tyrone automatically positioned himself where David could sleep on Tyrone's chest and in his arms. A light kiss brushed his chest, and the world fell away.

FIVE

It had been over a week since Tyrone last saw David. The time and distance were killing him. It seemed crazy that they lived so close yet felt so far apart. They talked on the phone and exchanged texts, but life kept pulling them in different directions. That ended today. After answering a house call at a property at the edge of David's, Tyrone found himself driving down David's driveway, as if his mind steered him in that direction with no real plan. Once again, Simone directed him to the stables.

Tyrone spotted Law as soon as he stepped through the door. "Hey, Law. How have you been?"

Law turned a bright smile his way. "Ty. Hey. I'm

good. David didn't tell me you were stopping by. It's good to see you."

Tyrone fought back a blush. "He didn't know I planned to visit."

"Those are the best surprises," Law said, his voice heavy with laughter. "If you go to the end stall on the left, you'll see a ladder leading to the loft. He's up there."

Tyrone flashed the man a smile before following his directions. He easily found the ladder and headed up the wooden rungs. David stood at a desk with his back to Tyrone. He held a clear container filled with what appeared to be water up to the light. Tyrone soaked up the sight of him. In worn jeans, an old-looking t-shirt, and well-worn work boots, it was the most dressed down Tyrone had ever seen the man. Tyrone realized something. David made every outfit look good. There was no place he didn't fit. From the tuxedo he'd worn to Jonah's wedding, the suit he'd worn when they met, to the outfit he wore now, he looked sexy as hell in everything.

"Just give me a minute to write down these numbers before I forget," David said without turning his way.

"No problem. I just thought I'd stop by since I was in the neighborhood."

David glanced over his shoulder. A smile lit his face. "Hey. I thought you were Law, coming to drag me out to the vineyard."

"Sorry. I know you're busy. Your neighbor called and asked if I could look at one of his cows, which was an odd request for me." Tyrone used the term neighbor loosely since David didn't have anyone near him for miles.

David bent over an open book on his desk and scribbled some notes before responding. "James Finn," he said, naming the neighbor. "He asked if I knew a good veterinarian. His retired earlier this year and the replacement he's been using since then has a habit of making him wait for hours and then doesn't show. I gave him your name." David turned his way. "I hope that's okay."

"It's fine. I'm always happy to have a new client. Plus, it was nice. I'm always stuck at the clinic." Tyrone turned in a circle and eyed the loft. One side held stacks of hay while the other half was an office. Nothing fancy. A desk, filing cabinet, and chair sat huddled together. The view was amazing. Two giant doors stood open, looking out over the land. From their height, Tyrone could make out the vineyard in the distance. There were also open fields and fenced spaces for the horses. "This place really is amazing." From left field, Tyrone felt completely outmatched. Everywhere he looked, as far as the eye could see, belonged to David. He couldn't begin to fathom the responsibility or having so much. He had absolutely nothing to offer David.

"You look sad."

If Tyrone had been looking David's way at the remark, maybe his tongue wouldn't have betrayed him. Unfortunately, David's claim came while Tyrone stared at everything he didn't have to offer. "You already have everything."

"I used to think so." Tyrone met David's gaze. With his weight braced on the edge of the desk and his feet crossed at the ankle, David watched him, as if waiting to have his attention before continuing. "And then I met you. That's when I realized how much I don't have. I'm not trying to scare you away," David added when Tyrone couldn't find the words to say he felt the same.

"I'm not sure that's possible."

David's entire demeanor changed, going from serious to playful. "You say that now, but I haven't started chasing you yet."

Tyrone couldn't stop smiling. "I'm not running."

David pushed away from the desk and closed the distance between them. "Maybe I should've said I haven't started laying siege yet. How long do I get to keep you?"

"How long do you want me?" Tyrone knew what David meant, but he couldn't let the moment pass. He might not get the opening again.

"I meant for today, but I don't think you want an answer to that. Don't forget, I'm trying not to scare you."

Gah. He never thought he'd be that guy, fishing for more. "Until an emergency arises. I'm on call," he clarified.

"I guess I'd better make the most of our time, then." David kicked the loft door closed, stopping anyone from ascending the ladder.

"You said you were needed at the vineyard."

David's arms encircled Tyrone's waist. He urged Tyrone closer. His smirk had Tyrone transfixed. "It's good to be the boss. I can choose you over everything every time."

"Every time?"

"I'm hoping," David said with a sexy-sounding chuckle.

The sound broke Tyrone. He snagged the back

of David's neck and hauled him forward. His mouth covered David's. The full bottom lip that made his mouth water was between his teeth. Hunger clawed at his gut. David cupped his face and deepened their kiss, taking control. Tyrone massaged every spot he could reach. David kissed and bit a path down Tyrone's throat, forcing him to suck air.

He couldn't stop his confession. "I woke up this morning with your name on my lips and my hand in my underwear."

David's kiss softened on Tyrone's neck, turning sweet. "You make me feel," he whispered against Tyrone's skin.

He needed to know exactly how he made David feel, but David didn't expound. David wrapped his arms around Tyrone's waist, pressed his cheek to Tyrone's chest, and held on. Something inside Tyrone expanded, filling him with an unnamed emotion. No one held him. Not anymore. He'd been single for years, settling for the occasional hook-up with people like Coy. A relationship seemed out of his reach with his busy schedule. David felt different. He felt real.

"You were my first thought this morning too," David said in a quiet voice. "I've missed you."

Tyrone's eyes fell closed. He soaked in the moment. "I've missed you too." Much more than he'd realized until they were in each other's arms. It wasn't fair to David to be with someone who couldn't find time for him. Tyrone would try harder. "What are you doing tomorrow night?"

"I'm sure nothing that can't be moved around. Why?"

"You should let me cook you dinner. Honestly, I'm not that great of a cook, but it would be just us and candle light."

"Sounds amazing to me. Just let me know a time. I'll be there."

It sounded like heaven to Tyrone. He'd move mountains to make it happen. "I'll text you an exact time after I look at my appointment book." As if speaking of appointments called to the universe, Tyrone's phone rang. "Damn. That'll be the office." It was always the office.

David backed away. He flashed a smile that looked faked to Tyrone. David might understand Tyrone's busy schedule more than others had, but there was a part of him that didn't like it. Tyrone could see it peeking out. "Text me when you can."

A knot tightened in Tyrone's chest. David wouldn't tolerate him forever whether he realized it yet or not. "I will. Kiss me again before I go. There's nothing that can't wait until after I've tasted you one more time." At the claim, David's smile turned genuine and sexy.

The distance between them disappeared again. Tyrone didn't hold back as he covered David's mouth. He poured all his longing into their kiss. The idea alone of losing David hurt. He didn't know why, after such a short amount of time together, he already wanted to panic at the thought of never seeing David again. They just fit. David made him want more. His phone stopped ringing and immediately started again. A groan rose in his throat as David pulled away.

"Go," David said, pushing him toward the ladder. Tyrone didn't get to judge his expression. David turned away too quickly. He lifted the loft door, freeing Tyrone. "You're needed elsewhere."

Did that mean he wasn't needed here? Tyrone bit his tongue to stop the question from escaping. "See you soon."

The fake smile was back. "I know. Now get lost. They're depending on you."

With a nod and a sense of dread, Tyrone descended the ladder. He almost made it back to his car. Coy stepped into his path. He didn't look much better than the last time Tyrone had seen him. His bruises had faded into a horrible yellow. Most likely, the cut across the bridge of his nose would scar. "Hey, Coy. How are you liking your new job?"

"Hey." Coy sounded different than usual. Sad. "It's a job. Law is a dick, but most men are, so that's nothing new. David seems nice, though."

Tyrone nodded. David was nice. There'd been no reason for David to take Coy in. Most people wouldn't have, much less given Coy a job, considering how fucked up his life obviously was. "He's pretty great."

"You should be careful."

Tyrone's eyebrows tried hitting his hairline at the warning. "What's that supposed to mean?"

Coy laughed, as if he'd meant the advice as a joke. "You know how these old men are. They don't think they have time to waste. You'll find yourself married after just a few of weeks of dating." Even though Coy was still smiling, there was a hint of malice in his eyes. For whatever reason, Coy had a lot of bitterness toward Tyrone.

Tyrone didn't try to fix it. "Well, there's worse things that could happen to me after a few weeks of dating, isn't there?" Without waiting to see if his words hit their mark, Tyrone walked away. Before he made it ten steps, there was a splash and a loud gasp behind him. Tyrone spun to find an outraged and dripping Coy.

Open hatred flashed in Coy's eyes as he turned on his water flinging assailant. "What the fuck, Law?"

Law's smile and laughing eyes said a lot about how much he'd enjoyed tossing a bucketful of water on Coy. "You looked like you needed cooling off. Just thought I'd lend a hand."

Tyrone pressed his lips together to keep from laughing and turned away. Law would have his hands full trying to keep Coy under control. He looked like he was up to the challenge.

WITH NOTHING but a small lamp to soften the darkness, David sat at his large oak desk and stared at the paperwork spread across it. In truth, he saw nothing. Ten had come and gone. David knew because he couldn't stop glancing at the face of his phone, waiting. No call or text came.

"Do you need any help?"

David glanced up at the intrusion. Coy lingered in the doorway, looking like he expected to be turned away. David wondered if he looked the same—rejected. "I don't know." A humorless laugh escaped him at the confession.

Coy moved closer, slowly at first. When David didn't stop him, he rolled an office chair to the side of David's desk and sat. "Your office smells like wood cleaner."

It was such an odd thing to say, David didn't know how to respond. So he said nothing.

Coy fidgeted, looking uncomfortable. "My grandmother works for a maid service. She helped raise me while my mom went to nursing school. She always smells like wood cleaner."

"I imagine Simone was in here dusting today," he responded absently as he checked his phone again.

"If he hasn't called by now, he won't. Tyrone doesn't believe in calling people after ten at night or before ten in the morning." When David's gaze moved Coy's way, Coy flinched. "Sorry. I shouldn't have said anything. I mean, I should pretend I don't know Tyrone. That's the fair thing to do." Coy blew out a sigh. "I'm sorry."

"Stop apologizing."

It was like Coy wasn't listening. "I don't want him, and I don't want you to think that I do. It's just that no one is ever nice to me. Tyrone was, which is probably why I don't really want him. It's just that you've been good to me too, and I don't want you to think I'm chasing him." Coy looked truly upset. "Sorry," he added again.

David didn't know how to make him stop except to talk so he couldn't. "He was supposed to check his schedule so we could make plans for tomorrow, but he hasn't texted me yet."

Coy nodded. "Since he's the only ER vet for miles in his area, he's always busy. Plus, it seems like once one emergency comes in, ten more come in right behind the first. He probably hasn't had time to check his schedule. In fact, five bucks says he won't even make it home tonight."

"He's killing himself." David didn't mean to sound quite so bitter, but there it was.

"Possibly," Coy said without a hint of judgment. "But what other choice does he have? You have everything. If you want to take a day off, it won't hurt you."

"I don't have everything." Even David heard the petulance in his tone. He didn't slow. "Besides, Tyrone is successful too."

Coy's gaze moved over David's face. His expression gave nothing away. "That success came with $250,000 in school loans. Add that to paying for his house, malpractice insurance, his business with all its extra expense, taxes, and paying his employees. If he takes a day off, he doesn't get paid. If he fails, he's not the only one who loses. His nurses have families. It's all on him. He has some high-skilled nurses. They can handle some of the minor appointments during the day. Other than that, it's all on him." Coy shrugged. "Ty claims it's passion driving him. Personally, I think it's desperation. He didn't have a rich family to put him through school, and they can't bail him out if he can't pay his bills. Ty is like most people. He's just doing the best he can with what's in front of him. But I think he really likes you. I've never seen him stop in the middle of his day to visit anyone."

David couldn't believe he was talking to Coy about this. He couldn't seem to stop. Like it or not, Coy had known Tyrone longer. "Sounds like there won't ever be a middle ground for us."

Coy shrugged. "You're definitely in an eighty-twenty relationship, but the twenty percent Tyrone can give you will always be amazing." He froze for a second as if a thought occurred to him. "Tyrone mentioned a volunteer at his office. Why don't you volunteer too when you're free? It's not the ideal date or anything, but you'd get to spend time together."

"Why are you sitting in the dark?" David's gaze shot to the door. Tyrone hovered in the open doorway. His gaze moved between David and Coy. "Simone let me in," he added when David didn't respond. "I took a chance you'd still be awake."

"I've got to do... something," Coy finished lamely as he hurried for the door. Tyrone moved out of his way, making room for him to pass. David noticed Coy kept his head down and didn't meet Tyrone's stare. He found the move odd, considering no one had managed to beat the fire out of Coy yet. David's happiness over Tyrone's appearance killed his curiosity.

"I'd given up on you for the night." David wanted the words back as soon as they left his lips.

Tyrone moved farther into the room. "Things got hectic when I made it to the office. The minute I was out of there, I remembered I hadn't texted you yet. I also realized I couldn't wait until tomorrow to see you again. If you're too tired for me, I won't stay long."

"Don't go." Even David heard the heat in his plea. Tyrone eyed him as if waiting for David to make the first move. David had no problem taking control. "Stay the night. We can figure out tomorrow when tomorrow comes."

Mischief lit Tyrone's eyes. "You'll have to lead the way. I've already forgotten how to get to your bedroom."

A smile overtook David. "In your defense, you were half asleep the last time I took you to bed."

Tyrone's mouth lifted in one corner, scorching David's skin. "I'm wide awake now. In fact," Tyrone said, closing them inside David's office. "Seeing you at a desk reminds me of all the thoughts I had when I saw you earlier today."

David fought back a chuckle. "I'm insulted. This desk is much nicer than the one at the stables."

The way Tyrone's gaze never wavered as he crossed the room had David's mouth watering. "Good. It'll be more comfortable for you when I fuck you on it."

Each breath David took came harder than the last as his desire increased by the second. His body ached for Tyrone. By the time Tyrone tugged him to his feet, David feared a little for Tyrone's skin. He planned to taste every inch. His lips tingled in anticipation. Tyrone made no move to kiss him. Instead, he held David's stare as he dragged David's shirt higher. His short fingernails scraped David's sides as the material moved up his body. David dutifully lifted his arms, allowing Tyrone to steal his shirt. The moment the material blinded him, Tyrone's mouth found his. David sucked in a gasp as their chests collided. His cock strained in his jeans, fighting to get closer to Tyrone. The shirt disappeared, freeing David. He clawed at Tyrone's scrubs. The thin material gave David the freedom to shove his hand inside Tyrone's underwear without preamble. He kneaded the man's erection, savoring the sounds Tyrone made against his lips. His feet left the floor. David's ass landed on the edge of the desk. He didn't let up. His teeth found Tyrone's bottom lip as he worked to steal Tyrone's pleasure. The world tilted, and David blinked at the ceiling in surprise. Something dug into his back, but it mattered not at all as Tyrone ripped open his jeans, setting David's erection free. A loud gasp echoed from the walls as Tyrone's hot mouth surrounded his cock, sucking hard. David scrambled for purchase. He scratched at the desk. At Tyrone's shoulders. Anything to hang on to so he could fuck Tyrone's skilled mouth. Insanity had him held in its grip. Before Tyrone, everything in his life had been muted. Now everything popped with color and felt twice as intense. David knew he was losing himself, falling too fast for someone who didn't really have space for him. Knowing changed nothing. David couldn't stop the forward march of his heart.

Tyrone froze. David fought a roar of denial. Blood pounded in his ears so loudly he almost missed the banging on the door. He fought his way back from the edge. Anger over the intrusion gave way to panic at Tyrone's expression. The raised voices on the other side of the door finally penetrated the lust fogging his brain.

"Fire! The stables are on fire."

David scrambled from the desk. He almost crippled himself trying to fix his jeans on the way to the door. When David threw open the door, he gave no fucks that he probably looked like he'd been doing exactly what he'd been doing. His skin still burned with unquenched desire. He could feel Tyrone at his back like they were connected in some invisible way. Law didn't wait for instructions once he had David's attention. He ran for the door with David on his heels. Outside, a crowd of workers were already gathered. Simone held the phone to ear, handling everything. David, Tyrone, and Coy leapt inside Law's waiting truck. Within minutes, they were outside the stables. Thankfully, it was only partially engulfed. The sound of panicked horses had Coy headed for the door—like he had no concern for his life.

Before he made three steps, Law jerked him off his feet. The boy seemed to hover mid-air for a moment before Law had him pinned to his chest. "Stop, idiot. What the hell is wrong with you? It's like you have no goddamn sense." Law's yelled admonishment could be heard over the wail of the smoke detectors.

"I can't stand here and do nothing," Coy shot back. He fought Law's tight hold.

"Each stall has an emergency release," David said, trying to cut through Coy's rage. "As soon as the alarm sounds, the outer doors on each stall opens, setting the horses free into the field." Coy finally stilled in Law's hold.

Law nodded, backing up David's words. "Animals are smart. No doubt they're scared, but they've got enough sense to get out."

Tyrone's hands landed on David's shoulders. He massaged, as if trying to lend David strength. "Once everything settles down, I'll grab my bag and check on the horses. I'll make sure they didn't hurt themselves in their race to escape."

David nodded as he watched the back half of his family stables burn. The place had been a part of his life his entire life. It was just a building, but it was his. "Thank you. Make sure you send me a bill for your time."

A loud snort sounded against his ear as Tyrone towed him back against his chest and wrapped his arms around him. "Don't be ridiculous."

Red lights flashed in the distance even as the flames slowly died beneath the onslaught of the sprinkler system.

"No way something small caused this," Law said, as if reading David's mind.

David nodded. "It had to be intentional. Otherwise, all our safety measures would have stopped the flames before they got out of control."

"Once this is handled, I'll take the Ranger out and look for any strange tracks."

At Law's offer, a hint of panic sneaked its way past the adrenaline pumping through David's veins. "Be careful. Don't go out alone or unarmed."

"I'll take this one with me," Law said, giving Coy a tiny shake and drawing attention to the fact he still held the man. "Since he seems so keen on doing something."

"You can let go of me now." Coy's voice sounded so dead David wasn't surprised when Law immediately released him.

"Just keeping your impulses in check. You obviously need a keeper."

Even though Coy didn't acknowledge Law's claim, his shoulders seemed to sag a little. David felt his pain. It did seem as if life had been on an ass-kicking roll lately. Personally, he was tired of it. He couldn't imagine how Coy felt.

SIX

WORDS COULDN'T EXPRESS HOW HAPPY TYRONE was to see Jonah again. He might've bounced a little while hugging him too tight. There was nothing about the man Tyrone hadn't missed from Jonah's stylishly messy brown hair to his lanky frame.

"I hadn't realized how much I'd come to depend on seeing you all the time until you weren't here. It feels like you've been on your honeymoon forever." Tyrone had also forgotten how incredibly gorgeous Jonah was, but his looks were almost muted in some way now. It was like Jonah seemed way too young for him, and he'd never noticed.

Jonah squeezed him back. "I missed you too. That's why I rushed over as soon as we got home. I figure you were close to your lunch break, so it would be okay to visit for a few. Tomorrow, I'll get back to helping you out. Today, I just wanted to see your gorgeous face." Jonah cupped his cheeks and eyed him as if he really had missed the sight of Tyrone.

Tyrone took his hand and led him inside his office. "Come on. I want to hear about every minute."

A sexy laugh tumbled behind him. "You really don't. I, on the other hand," Jonah said, sounding like he knew a secret, "would like to hear all about what's going on with David."

Rearranging his features into some semblance of innocence, Tyrone sat behind his desk. "What's that supposed to mean?"

Jonah pulled his chair up close to the desk and sat. "Don't play dumb. David called twice while I was away to check in."

Tyrone stamped down the urge to ask what he'd said. Fuck. He really wanted to know. To hell with playing it cool. It was Jonah. "I really like him."

"Yay," Jonah cheered, clapping and bouncing in his seat. "I was a little worried you wouldn't have anything in common when John suggested the two of you pair up for the wedding. Of course, John knows his stuff. He called it."

"Called what?"

"That David would sweep you off your feet," Jonah said, sounding as if the answer should be obvious. "The moment we saw the two of you together, John leaned over and whispered we'd be at your wedding next."

Tyrone rubbed the back of his neck, feeling exposed. "I don't know about that. We haven't been seeing each other long." Tyrone blew out a sigh. A smile that was out of his control pulled at his cheeks. "But he's amazing. I'm feeling way out of my comfort zone because we're both incredibly busy people. It's killing me trying to find ways to see him."

"Hmmm," Jonah said, pressing his lips together. "That will take some thinking, but I'll help you figure it out." A knowing smile stretched Jonah's lips. "Don't stress too hard, though. He really likes you. You should've heard him. I couldn't wait to see for myself if you feel the same. Now that I'm looking at it, I'm doubly excited for you both."

A low knock sounded on the open door. Tyrone and Jonah looked that way. Coy lingered in the doorway, holding two large paper bags and looking unsure of his welcome. "Um, hi."

"Hey," Tyrone said back.

"David sent me over. He has meetings all day, but he wanted to make sure you got lunch."

Tyrone eyed the large bags while trying not to meet Jonah's knowing look. "That looks like a hell of a lot of food."

A reluctant-looking smile stretched Coy's lips. "I think he didn't want anyone at your office to feel left out."

It couldn't have been more obvious Coy expected to be tossed out at any moment. Tyrone motioned toward his desk. "Let's see what you've brought."

Coy cast Jonah a shy smile before slipping past him to set the bags on Tyrone's desk. "I didn't look, so I don't know what's in there."

"Let's look together." Tyrone came to his feet and pulled out a few containers. "Most of the staff went to lunch earlier." Tyrone peeked inside one of the boxes. "You should stay and get in on this. It looks like baked chicken and red potatoes in this one."

Coy took a step backward and looked in every direction except Tyrone's. "It's okay. You should take the leftovers home."

Tyrone hated that Coy obviously felt unwanted, or like he was intruding. He couldn't let Coy continue feeling so alone in the world. Tyrone pasted on his brightest smile. "Seriously, Coy. Stay."

Adding power to his argument, Jonah pushed a chair closer to Coy with his foot and smiled. Coy's gaze moved between them. He still looked uncomfortable, but he sat. Coy swiped his hands on his thighs. He stared at Tyrone's desk. Even when Tyrone popped open a box and set it in front of Coy, he didn't lift his chin or move to touch the food. Tyrone tried handing a box to Jonah, but he waved it away.

"I can't stay."

With a shrug, Tyrone sat and dug into his food. It was delicious. He fought the urge to hum in delight. The only thing stopping him from orgasmically enjoying his meal was Jonah. His light brown gaze never wavered from staring a hole in the side of Coy's face. Coy was visibly trying not to notice.

"What happened to your face?"

Tyrone froze with his fork raised halfway to his mouth. His gaze moved between them, wondering if Coy would snap under the combined pressure of Jonah's stare and question. Coy kept his gaze locked on his food.

Jonah poked him in the arm. "Hey, Boy. What happened to your face?"

Tyrone bit the inside of his cheek to keep from laughing. Jonah wasn't that much older than Coy.

Hearing Jonah refer to Coy as Boy was too much. It seemed Coy thought so too since he didn't ignore him this time.

His eyes flashed with defiance when he looked Jonah's way. "Exactly what you're thinking, I imagine."

Jonah didn't back down or flinch. "Did you get a restraining order?"

Tyrone was a bit ashamed he hadn't thought to ask. He'd been preoccupied trying to juggle his life.

Coy looked away. His expression punched Tyrone in the gut. "That's never mattered in the past."

This wasn't the first time. Tyrone wondered if he'd ever breathe properly again. Ex or not, Coy didn't deserve this. Tyrone should've tried harder to help. Coy probably needed counseling or something.

Thankfully, Jonah didn't seem to mind butting his way into Coy's life. "I know someone who could break his kneecaps for you."

Coy met Jonah's stare. He looked a bit too interested. "What would it cost me?"

Jonah waved a dismissive hand. "I can afford it. Just let me take care of everything."

The smile that lit Coy's face made the crazy

conversation that could be used against them in court worthwhile. "I'm Coy."

Jonah dipped his chin, acknowledging Coy's introduction. "Jonah. So, you work for Mr. Baker?"

Coy nodded. "He recently took me in."

"Lucky," Jonah said brightly. "I love David. He walked me down the aisle at my wedding."

"Oh, yeah. You must be the volunteer Ty mentioned getting married a couple of weeks ago."

Jonah's smile brightened. "Yep. That's me. Speaking of which, I need to head out. John and I are sending out thank you gifts today."

"John and Jonah. That's adorable."

Jonah released a loud and happy-sounding sigh at Coy's claim. "Isn't it, though? It was nice meeting you, Coy. Don't be a stranger." He looked Tyrone's way. "See you tomorrow, sweetie."

Tyrone winked. "See you, babe."

The moment Jonah left them alone, Coy struck. "On the topic of thank you gifts, you should send me back to David with a note or something for this lunch."

Coy confused the hell out of Tyrone. "What are you up to?"

"Nothing." Coy sounded a little too innocent for Tyrone's liking. "You're dating someone for real now.

This isn't just a hookup. It's time for you to put in some effort."

Tyrone's eyebrows shot up. "Are you saying I don't put any effort into relationships?"

The way Coy shrugged screamed the answer should be obvious. Worry wormed its way in. Had David complained about him working too much? An image of Coy and David, sitting in the dark and talking, sprang to mind. Their conversation had seemed intimate when Tyrone had appeared the other night. Tyrone hadn't checked his schedule the way he'd promised. It was possible David felt neglected. David wasn't the type to complain, especially when it was work keeping them apart.

Tyrone pushed to his feet and headed for the supply closet. He found a small brown paper bag and stuffed some condoms and lube inside. They were supposed to be for medical purposes but whatever. Back at his desk, Coy picked at his food while Tyrone found a scratch pad and wrote a quick note to David. As he dropped the note inside the bag and rolled it closed, he hoped Coy didn't go snooping.

"Here," he said, passing the bag to Coy. "You're not returning empty handed."

Coy accepted the bag. He set it at his feet and

went back to moving the food around inside its box. Tyrone wasn't sure any of it actually found its way inside his mouth. Coy had always been a small guy, but he looked like he'd lost weight to Tyrone. A hint of concern ate at him.

"How are you holding up?"

Coy's gaze shot to his, obviously surprised at the inquiry. "Fine."

Tyrone nodded, even though it was a bullshit answer. "How are you liking it, working for David?"

One of Coy's shoulders lifted in a half shrug. "I can't complain." He looked around, not meeting Tyrone's stare as he swiped his palms on his thighs. "I should probably head back. Law already doesn't trust me. I'm sure he's ready to send the police out for his truck."

"Why wouldn't Law trust you?"

Coy shrugged again. "He just doesn't."

It was probably because Coy looked like a man who'd been beaten within an inch of his life. That reeked of trouble. "He obviously trusts you enough to lend you his truck."

"Maybe he shouldn't," Coy muttered under his breath as he stood. Before Tyrone could think of a way to respond, Coy scooped up the paper bag and met his stare. He looked tired. Black marks smudged beneath his eyes, making him seem years older. Unhappiness etched his every feature. "I'll make sure David gets your gift."

Tyrone nodded. "Hey," he said before Coy could get away. "You know I'm around if you need me, right?"

Coy's expression never changed. His eyes weren't exactly dead. It was more like Coy was faded. "Why would I need you?"

"Everyone needs someone."

"Not me," Coy said, turning away, and stealing Tyrone's chance to argue. His appetite fled as he watched Coy walk away. He preferred the angry side of Coy. At least he'd always known that version of Coy was still fighting. He wasn't sure that was true any longer. Before Tyrone had time to think things over, Coy reappeared in the doorway. He looked even more exhausted and Tyrone hadn't thought that possible.

"It seems I need you after all."

"What's wrong?"

Coy's chest expanded on a deep breath and his gaze skirted away. "All four tires on Law's truck have been slashed."

Fuck. Tyrone was tired on Coy's behalf. There was no telling how long Coy had been silently living this way. He closed his food box and repacked the bag. "Let's go." Who knew? Maybe he'd get to see David sometime today along the way. On the drive to David's, Coy called Law. He took turns chewing on the side of his thumbnail and profusely apologizing. Tyrone couldn't hear Law's side of the conversation. Part of him wished he couldn't hear Coy's either. He'd never seen someone so defeated before. When they made it to the house, Law was already waiting outside. He didn't look upset as they climbed from the car.

Tyrone spoke first, saving Coy from issuing another apology. "How do you want to handle this?"

Law stood and brushed off his ass from where he'd been sitting on the front steps. His white t-shirt stretched tight across his broad shoulders at the movement. Law bent and picked up his straw cowboy hat. "If you don't mind driving me over there, I know a guy who owns a tire shop. He'll meet me with a tow truck."

"Sounds good," Tyrone said, heading back to the car.

Law opened the passenger side door. With his head down, looking like life had beat him down, Coy moved for the back door.

"Hello," Law called, dragging out the word and

snagging Coy's attention. Tyrone swallowed down a laugh as Law obnoxiously motioned toward the door he held open for Coy. "I'm sitting in the back." He shook his head as if he didn't understand Coy at all. Coy looked strangely suspicious as he slid into the passenger seat. Law shook his head again as he closed the door and headed for the back. An odd thought hit Tyrone, but he kept it to himself.

The moment they were on the road, Coy broke. He spun in his seat and focused on Law. "I'm so sorry about your tires. You can take the cost out of my check. I don't know what happened. Seriously, I'm so, so sorry."

"Stop apologizing all the time," Law grumbled. "I don't need your money. It's just one of those things."

Tyrone hung on every word exchanged between them. Law was gruff and not especially friendly with Coy, but there was still something in his tone Tyrone couldn't quite put his finger on. There was a nosy little bitch inside him that wanted to speculate and know one hundred and three percent of the details.

"It's one of my things," Coy muttered as he faced forward again and went back to staring at his lap.

"I have security cameras," Tyrone offered. "If someone slashed those tires in my parking lot, the video will be saved in my cloud."

Neither Coy nor Law acknowledged his claim. With an internal shrug, Tyrone concentrated on driving while simultaneously wondering what David was doing right that second. Damn. He was dealing with whatever hell was plaguing Coy's life, but David still ruled his every thought. It seemed he should feel a little guilty, but he couldn't shake the constant happiness David brought to his life.

A cellphone rang in the backseat. "It's David," Law said before answering. Tyrone bit his bottom lip, trying to hide his excitement. David was right there. On the phone. Just feet away. "Hello? Hey. We're on our way now. Ty says he has security cameras." Tyrone fought the urge to stare in the rear-view mirror like a crazy person. "Okay. I'll let him know. Talk to you in a few." Law tucked his phone in his front pocket. "David says he'll meet you at the office to look at the cameras with you."

Tyrone nodded, hoping to hide his excitement.

Coy turned his head and stared out the opposite window. Tyrone found himself driving a little faster. When the office came into view, he spotted David already waiting for him. It was like the weight of the world lifted from his shoulders. David gave him more than happiness; he took away the pressure of living. It was as if Tyrone could hand his life over to the man and know he didn't have to worry for a while. When David wasn't around, all Tyrone did was stress over every detail. No one knew. His business. All the bills. Being in charge and responsible for everyone; it was dragging him down and choking him. Some days he didn't know how much longer he could tolerate the nonstop grind. It had started as passion and determination. Now it was a necessity and he felt himself buckling.

Without a thought or care for anyone else, Tyrone leapt from the car. David's smile kept Tyrone moving in his direction. Then David pushed away from his car, meeting Tyrone halfway. Tyrone's heart skipped a beat. His mouth found David's with no plan. He felt David's smile against his lips.

"Hey, gorgeous."

A chuckle rose in Tyrone's throat. "Hey. I guess I've missed you a little."

The way David's gaze moved over his features made Tyrone wonder how much of his feelings showed in his expression. "I think we should talk while looking through that footage."

Damn. That didn't sound ominous at all. "Okay." Tyrone motioned toward the building. "After you."

"We'll wait on my friend to get here," Law said his voice heavy with laughter.

Tyrone glanced his way and nodded, letting Law know he'd heard. Thanks to David's "let's talk" comment, Tyrone had a lump in his throat, stifling his voice. David had a nice ass, though. Tyrone couldn't tear his eyes away as he followed him inside. He wasn't ready for David to give up on him. Not yet. Tyrone wasn't sure he'd ever be ready for that. Unfortunately, he had a bad feeling he was about to find out.

THE WAY TYRONE looked as he'd jumped from the car in a hurry to get to him had David's mind a mess. He wasn't the type to waste his time, wondering if someone felt anything for him. Tyrone didn't try to hide his emotions. Everything he felt showed in his eyes. David wanted more. For every ounce of excitement Tyrone showed, David craved ten more. His heart was greedy like that. As he led the way to Tyrone's office, the ache he felt to have Tyrone grew until his hands itched to be on Tyrone's skin.

The moment they cleared Tyrone's office doorway, David pushed the door closed and found Tyrone's mouth. He bit the man's bottom lip and sucked on it in apology before delving inside. Their tongues clashed and stroked. He tore off his jacket and tossed it aside, going back for more. Tyrone chuckled against his lips. "I thought you wanted to talk."

David kissed him deep before bothering to answer. "I am talking. You hear me loud and clear. I can feel it." He knew it was true. They got each other. They weren't playing. This wasn't for the fun of it. They were building something real.

Tyrone pulled away and touched his forehead to David's. He visibly sucked air, trying to catch his breath. His eyes opened. He looked turned on and sexy as fuck. "Jesus. You're the first person who's ever made me wish I had nothing else to do but you."

The instant smile that popped to David's lips at the confession was out of his control. "Same."

"We should probably check out that camera."

David nodded, squishing their foreheads together. They automatically reached for each other. Their fingers linked. "I imagine Law is impatient to know if Coy's life just exploded all over his truck."

Tyrone pulled a face, proving he felt the same as David. Poor Coy. No one deserved this craziness. "Come on. It's all digital. I just need to log in and check any movement around that time. It'll only take a moment." Tyrone moved to his desk and woke his computer. After a few clicks, he had a list of times and motions pulled up on the screen. He clicked one. Nothing but a shadow on the pavement showed and then something covered the screen. "Damn. He covered the camera." Tyrone clicked the next time entry. It was the same. The camera was still covered. They exchanged a glance. As one, they headed outside and around the corner. Law and Coy eyed them as they passed. They didn't slow until the camera came into view. A black t-shirt draped over the camera. Tyrone pulled it down and held the material up for inspection. It was an old metal band's t-shirt. Coy and Law appeared on their heels. David glanced over his shoulder. Coy's face said it all.

David nodded toward the shirt. "Do you recognize that?"

Coy dipped his chin in a jerky nod. He visibly swallowed but didn't meet anyone's gaze. "It's mine." David didn't need to ask how it ended up covering the camera. Coy had abandoned his things for his safety's sake. Only his psycho ex would have access to his clothes. Coy took a deep breath and finally met David's stare. "I'd give you my notice, but I think it's best I go away now before you end up with anymore damaged property or worse. You can keep any money owed to me. I know it's not enough to cover anything, but I don't have anything else to offer right now. As soon as I find another job, I'll make payments or something until you're paid back for everything that's happened since you took me in."

Before David could think of a thing to say, Law released a loud curse and walked away. Coy immediately dropped his chin again, going back to staring at the ground. The way he blinked had David worried about how close to the edge he might be. Still, he didn't think pity would help Coy's mental state.

"You're not going anywhere." At David's hard tone, Coy focused on him once more. David didn't back down. "If you want to pay me back, then go help Law and get back to work."

Coy blinked. "Yes, sir."

David waited until Coy was out of earshot before releasing his breath. His gaze slid Tyrone's way. Tyrone's gorgeous light brown eyes were locked on him. When their gazes met, Tyrone's mouth lifted in one corner. "You're a good man."

"Am I?" David asked, not feeling too sure. "Because I kind of want to find this fucker and mail him home in pieces."

Tyrone's smile grew. "That's what makes you a

good man." He shook his head and his smile fell. "What do you plan to do? You realize there's a good chance this guy is who burned your stables. This can't continue. He's obviously crazy enough to kill someone."

David blew out a sigh. "I suppose I'll try to do things the legal way. Point the police in his direction. Honestly, though, I don't expect there's much they can do without any real evidence." David eyed the building, and a chill raced down his spine. "The thing is, I think he's locked on to you. I mean, the fire started after you showed up the other night. Between that and today, I think it's you he's watching to get to Coy."

"How would he know me?" Tyrone didn't sound exactly disbelieving, but neither did he sound convinced.

"I don't know." David looked around again. It was almost like he could feel the eyes upon them. "I just have a bad feeling about this whole thing. Coy doesn't behave like someone who walked away after a single incident. He acts like someone who knows he's in real danger." He held Tyrone's stare. "I think you should stay with me too for a while. At least until this guy moves on to his next obsession."

A line appeared between Tyrone's eyebrows.

"Do you know how inconvenient it'll be for you to have me staying with you? I might be home at two in the afternoon or four in the morning. You'll never feel like you've slept." Despite Tyrone's attempt to discourage him, David thought his claims sounded like heaven. Tyrone's frown deepened. "Why are you smiling?"

David shook his head. "You referred to my house as home. It had a nice ring to it falling from your lips. Truthfully, I'm thinking you should be terrified of me."

"I'm not." The surety in Tyrone's tone punched David in the heart.

"Does that mean you'll put my mind at ease and stay with me?"

Tyrone eyed him for a moment in silence. His chin dipped in a barely perceptible nod. "I think it's safe to say there's not much I wouldn't do for you."

Possessiveness roared through David. "Go tell Kelly you're leaving for the day."

The frown reappeared. "I'm not really in a position to do that."

David bit back his irritation. "Either you trust me to always look out for your welfare or you don't. Do you trust me or not?"

"Of course."

The way Tyrone didn't hesitate made David proud. "Then go tell your staff you're leaving. I'll leave my car with Law so they're not stranded while we head over to your house. You can grab whatever you need for an extended stay."

Tyrone still looked like he'd narrowly missed being sideswiped by a fast-moving train, but he nodded. David followed on his heels barely holding back his self-satisfied grin. He hated what was happening to Coy but loved the effect it had on his life. Soon enough, Tyrone would realize he wasn't getting away.

SEVEN

FROM HIS SPOT ON THE BED, DAVID WATCHED
Tyrone put away his stuff. Even while wearing
nothing more than pajama pants, he was overheated.
There was something primal about sharing his space
with Tyrone—like a caveman providing shelter.
Truthfully, though, David had way more space than
one person needed. He hadn't been forced to
rearrange a thing for Tyrone. There were empty
drawers and closet space. Counter space in the
bathroom. His bed was definitely big enough for two.
Not that he intended to give Tyrone any breathing
room there. Speaking of which, his patience was
wearing thin.

"You should leave that for now and come here."

Tyrone glanced over his shoulder. "Do you think

so? You'll be tripping over my things for god knows how long, because I'm not likely to have another day off anytime soon."

"Then I'll put it away for you. Come here." This time, his tone left no room for argument.

Tyrone's eyes flashed with humor as he crossed the room. He stopped a foot from the bed and made no move to reach for David. "Here?"

With a laugh that sounded evil even to his ears, David slipped down the bed and rearranged his body until his head hung off the edge of the mattress. "That'll work," he said, reaching for Tyrone's hips and urging him forward.

Chin down and heated gaze locked on David, Tyrone didn't argue as David pulled the knot loose on his pajama pants. His position was awkward, but he knew it wouldn't be for long. Tyrone shuffled forward as David set his growing erection free. Damn, he loved the way Tyrone's cock felt in his hands. Tyrone ran his hands down David's chest before moving back to his neck. He gently cupped David's chin, and he led his dick to David's lips. He brushed his crown across David's bottom lip. David opened for him. His cock slid across David's tongue, hitting the back of his throat. David swallowed.

Tyrone sucked in a sharp breath. The sound ricocheted off the walls.

"Damn. I want you to fly too." Tyrone shoved David's pants down and palmed David's cock. A moan rose in David's throat. "Holy shit, David. Do that again." David didn't need to be told. The way Tyrone toyed with him already had him on the edge of insanity. Mewling sounds escaped him as he sucked, doing his damnedest to please Tyrone. He needed Tyrone's orgasm and his happiness. David craved Tyrone's every emotion. He needed them to be real. Tyrone openly fucked David's mouth, taking what he wanted. "Oh my god. I don't know why you affect me like this. You always take me from one high to the next." David couldn't even think. Between Tyrone's hands and his words, he was on fire. His throat burned. David didn't care. All he cared about was Tyrone. "I shouldn't want so much so fast. You make me dream." David's eyes stung at the confession. He knew it was heat of the moment babbling, but sometimes those were the most heartfelt admissions. The tongue was unguarded. Hearts were exposed.

The stroking of his cock quickened. David's back arched. His hips lifted, seeking more. Everything fell away except the growing pressure. Each second, he wound tighter. Tyrone's movements turned desperate. He pushed deep. Hot cum filled David's mouth. A strangled cry left Tyrone. The sound stole David's orgasm. He held Tyrone's hips, licking the mess away as Tyrone worked every twitch from David. Tyrone backed away and bent, capturing David's lips. With the flavor of Tyrone's cum still coating his mouth, Tyrone switched between deep kisses and sweet brushes of lips. David fought for air. Words choked him. He couldn't recall a time he'd cared so much about anyone. He didn't have any living blood relatives anymore and his life had been filled with nothing but work. Before Tyrone, he'd never felt the least bit incomplete. Now he felt empty anytime Tyrone wasn't around. David scared himself. Tyrone should be terrified of him because David wouldn't stop pursuing all of him until Tyrone felt the same emptiness without him.

"Come to bed with me," David begged.

Tyrone brushed a kiss across the bridge of David's nose. "Let me clean you up first. Then I promise I'll spend the rest of the night petting you."

A soft laugh escaped David at Tyrone's choice of words. He settled down and watched as Tyrone disappeared inside the bathroom and came back with a towel. Tyrone gently swiped at his skin, cleaning away the mess. He kept his gaze locked on his task. An odd thought, apropos to nothing, hit David.

"How is it that a vet who obviously loves animals doesn't own a single animal?"

A smile snapped to Tyrone's lips. He tossed the towel aside and urged David over in the bed. As he climbed onto the mattress, he tugged at the covers, making David comfortable. "At least once a day, I have to put other people's pets to sleep. It's heartbreaking. You'd think I'd eventually harden against it, but I don't. Between that and never being home, I don't think I would make a good pet dad." A pained look passed over Tyrone's features. "Honestly, I'm worried I'll be a disappointment to you too. I've never tried juggling like this before." Tyrone's mouth lifted in one corner in a sexy crooked smile. "I've also never cared this much about making someone else happy. It may not seem like it, but I'm trying hard for you."

After shifting onto his knees, David tumbled Tyrone onto his back and straddled him. He covered Tyrone's body with his, crossed his hands over Tyrone's chest, and set his chin on his hands. With Tyrone pinned right where David wanted him, he held Tyrone's stare. "You're not trying alone. That's the awesome thing about being me. I can drop everything and come to you, and I will. If I'm feeling neglected, I'll follow you around and invade your space." Tyrone's smile grew with David's every claim. David didn't stop. "I'm one hundred percent serious. You'll beg me to go away."

"I look forward to reaching that point."

"Good." It would probably happen sooner rather than later.

Tyrone ran his fingers through David's hair. His expression turned serious as his gaze moved over David's features. He stroked David's face, tracing his cheekbones and the line of his nose before brushing his fingertips along David's lips. "I want to recognize you even in the dark," he whispered, squeezing David's heart. David turned his head and kissed Tyrone's palm. His eyes fell closed as he inhaled Tyrone's scent. With the slightest pressure, Tyrone urged David closer until he could claim his lips. There was nothing sexual about the kiss. It was sweet and filled with promise. In that moment, David caught a glimpse of their future together. It was beautiful.

EIGHT

THE SMELL OF HORSES, HAY, AND CRISP AIR filled Tyrone's nostrils. A steady heartbeat filled his eardrums. He moved the stethoscope lower. Steady air whooshed from the horse's lungs, sounding clear. Tyrone ran his hand down her spine.

"Sweet girl." Abby had been battling a cold but sounded good. The runny nose and cough had cleared. Her appetite was slowly returning. Tyrone felt safe telling David she was on the mend. Between Abby getting better, the stables getting set back to rights, and no new drama, everything was perfect, except for the fact that everything was perfect. That meant Tyrone really didn't have a reason to keep staying at David's, except he wanted to stay with David. Hiding in Abby's stall seemed the perfect place to think. Weeks without an incident was long enough to assume things had blown over. It hadn't occurred to Tyrone that he should leave until he'd checked his bank account. His house payment had cleared overnight. He was paying for a house, one he hadn't seen other than a quick drive by in the past month. He was an adult. This wasn't his home. The last thing Tyrone wanted was to overstay his welcome. Not that David had complained. It had been David's idea for him to stay there in the first place. Still, Tyrone had a whole other life elsewhere. Lately, it seemed he spent more time at David's than he did at the office. That was something that had never happened. He wasn't having any problems paying his bills despite the change, thanks to David's neighbors constantly calling him for help. Surely there was a middle ground between this life and his old one. If so, he needed to find it quick.

"Everyone else around here manages to get done on time. What's your excuse?"

At the admonishment, Tyrone shifted positions as quietly as possible to bring the people behind the voices into sight. Law was hovering over Coy while Coy swept.

"I'm already off the clock," Coy said quietly. He

didn't look Law's way. "This just needed to be done, so I'm doing it."

"Save it for tomorrow, then. People don't work off the clock around here."

Coy's shoulders fell. He still didn't look Law's way as he set the broom in the corner, abandoning the chore. A spike of pity hit Tyrone. He'd noticed Law seemed harder on Coy than he was anyone else —like he couldn't do anything right. Tyrone opened the stall door, making his presence known. Two sets of eyes swung his way. A welcoming smile lit Law's face while Coy immediately looked away.

"How's Abby doing?"

"She's good," Tyrone said, answering Law's question. "I think it's safe to say she'll be fine."

"Good. I'll let David know when he gets home, and I give him my report for the day."

Tyrone nodded. His gaze slid Coy's way. Coy was easing toward the door as if hoping to make his escape without notice. "Hey, Coy. If you're not busy, I have to head to the office for a couple of appointments. Would you like to help?"

The hopeful glint in Coy's eyes let him know he'd made the right choice. Coy needed out from underneath the oppressive judgment of others for a little while. Still, he didn't let his guard down. "Sure. If you need me."

"I could use the extra set of hands. Jonah usually only volunteers Monday through Wednesday, and never at night. That leaves me doing these after-hours appointments alone."

Coy nodded. "Okay."

Tyrone pulled his key fob from his pocket and tossed it Coy's way. "You can head to the car. I'll grab my stuff and meet you in a second."

With a dip of his chin, Coy headed for the door. The moment he was gone, Tyrone focused on Law. "He's just bored. I'll keep him busy for a few hours. If you need him back before then, give the office a call."

"Meh," Law said, sounding indifferent. "He's done for the day. I have to stay on him or he'll work off the clock nonstop. I don't know how else to make him understand this is his home too. It's okay to relax occasionally. Not everything is his responsibility. It's like he's still trying to atone for the fire and the tires, neither of which is his fault. Not really." Law shrugged. "He doesn't relax. Not ever."

A chuckle escaped Tyrone. He slapped Law across the back. "He won't have a choice at my office. I don't really have anything for him to do." A loud laugh burst from Law. The sound made him smile. "See you, Law. Stay out of trouble."

"There's no fun in that," Law called at his back as Tyrone headed out. Tyrone fought his laughter. Coy was waiting in the passenger seat. Tyrone tossed his bag in the backseat before sliding behind the wheel.

"Do you have any stops you need to make while we're out? It has to be a pain having no way to leave this place."

Coy shrugged. "David has work trucks we're allowed to use. Not that I have anywhere to go."

Tyrone shook his head as he steered his way down the long drive. "You're not dead yet, Coy. Go to a club. Meet someone nice, or don't. Listen to the music. Dance. Be young."

An ugly-sounding snort escaped Coy. "No thanks. I prefer the quiet. If I need noise, all I have to do is stand still. Law will come along and yell at me."

He carefully kept his gaze locked on the road. "Yeah. What's up with that? I noticed he seems to be unusually fond of correcting you."

"Most people are." Coy didn't sound upset over it, merely resigned—like it was his lot in life.

"Tell him to kiss your ass. You don't owe anyone anything."

"That's not true." Coy's automatic denial was more forceful than Tyrone expected. It was definitely more passionate than Coy had been in a while. "I owe David everything. The least I can do is try to make Law happy, even if it seems impossible."

Tyrone released a slow breath. He didn't know how to handle this. Honestly, it wasn't his issue to handle. Coy needed time. Eventually, he'd go back to the carefree and fun-loving person he'd been when they'd first met. All Tyrone could do was let it happen naturally.

Two hours after arriving at his office, Coy proved to be a great help. Normally, Tyrone paid a cleaning service to come in every night. As he watched Coy move from room to room cleaning, he wondered if Coy wouldn't do a better job. Not that he was unhappy with his cleaning service. He just liked the idea of paying someone he knew and who needed the money.

Coy walked past the exam room door. Tyrone called out, stopping him. "Hey, Coy. Can I talk to you a minute?"

He snagged the doorframe and popped his head into the room. "Sure. What's up?"

Tyrone waved him inside. "You're doing a great job." Coy smiled for the first time in what felt like forever. Tyrone kept going. "I really appreciate your help. How do you feel about doing this as a second job?"

"You're my friend. I don't expect to get paid."

Tyrone snagged a rolling stool with his foot and sat. "Right now, I pay a cleaning service to come in at night Monday through Friday. The place looks better after just two hours of you cleaning due to boredom than when they do it for pay. If you're interested, I'd rather pay you."

Coy worried at his bottom lip. "Can I think about it?"

"Sure." As the word left his lips, a large man in a black t-shirt and ripped jeans appeared at Coy's back. He towered over Coy by a foot. His arms were the size of Tyrone's thighs. The guy's dark hair was a mess. He looked like he'd been running his fingers through it. "We're actually closed right now? Do you have an emergency?"

Coy glanced over his shoulder at Tyrone's question. It was a quick look, but it was enough to send him scrambling. He wasn't fast enough before his feet left the floor. Shock made Tyrone slow to react as Coy was carried from the room like a struggling doll.

"Just retrieving what's mine," the guy said,

sounding ridiculously calm for someone abducting a person.

"Let go, King. I'm not going anywhere with you."

Tyrone tossed aside the file he'd been going over and sprinted after the pair. He didn't have time to consider the best course of action. Protecting Coy was the only thought in his head. "Drop him."

King kept moving, seemingly oblivious to Coy's struggle and Tyrone's demands. Before Tyrone closed the distance between them, Coy landed a solid boot heel to King's kneecap. "I'm not going."

A roar of outrage bounced from the walls. King's fist collided with Coy's face so fast Tyrone didn't see the punch coming. The sound the hit made as it landed and the way Coy's head snapped back was something Tyrone knew he'd remember the rest of his life. Coy didn't go down, proving he could take a hit. He fought back, managing to get in a few blows.

Tyrone tried inserting himself between the pair while still moving toward the door. The only real plan he had was to get King out of the building and a door locked between them. He didn't have time to think of anything rational.

"I'm not your fucking punching bag anymore. Get the fuck out." Coy punctuated each yelled word with a swing. A few glanced off Tyrone in his attempt to break things up.

"If you're not mine, you're not anyone's, especially no rich doctor. You're too fucking stupid for anyone else to want you for anything other than a piece of ass, but I'll be goddamned if I'll let anyone else have you." The light reflected off something in King's hand. Tyrone didn't have time to consider his actions. He pushed Coy behind him. Everything flashed before his eyes, yet he had time for a thousand thoughts. He wondered how Coy had survived living like this for so long. David's image rose to mind. He hoped Jonah didn't randomly decide to drop by. It had been months since he'd talked to his brother. He should've called his mom while he had the chance. A boom rang out. It struck him as odd that a sound could unbalance him to the point of nearly knocking him off his feet. An oddly satisfied smile touched King's lips as he turned to walk away. He stuffed a gun in the back of his pants as he went before covering it with his shirt. Coy's hands tugged at his body. His lips moved, but Tyrone couldn't hear a thing. He blinked at the lights, confused as to why they were in his line of sight when they should be above his head. They dimmed. His heartbeat pounded in his ears. The air thickened, making it harder for him to breathe. Reality slipped away.

THERE WAS a crack in the wall. It was such an insignificant thing to catch and hold David's attention. That damn crack held David's lungs hostage, robbing him of air. How could a place that didn't tend to their walls fix Tyrone? He should have Tyrone transferred to a better hospital. One that wasn't falling apart around him.

"Mr. Baker."

David turned his head. Jonah was headed his way with John in tow. David thought to come to his feet, but his body refused to listen. He couldn't feel anything in his limbs.

Jonah filled the chair beside him. David's gaze moved over his concerned features. He wanted to comfort him. Jonah was Tyrone's friend. No doubt, Jonah was on the edge of falling apart. His throat wouldn't work. "Oh, sweetie," Jonah cooed, pulling him into a hug. The lump in his throat doubled in size. "Has there been any update?"

David shook his head. A couple lingered behind Jonah, looking every bit as worried. Jonah motioned toward the pair. "This is Charlie and Tarah, Tyrone's parents."

At the introduction, David managed to push to his feet. "I'm sorry we're meeting under these circumstances," David said, reaching out to shake their hands. "I don't know if you know who I am."

Tarah cut him off. "Yes. David. Ty has told me all about you. He's been trying to make time for us to meet, but I understand you both have crazy schedules. I never expected—" Her voice broke.

David motioned toward the chair he'd vacated. "Please have a seat. He's still in surgery. I don't think I can sit anymore." Tyrone looked like Tarah. They had the same beautiful dark skin tone. Tyrone had gotten his dad's nose and eyes. He couldn't stop switching his gaze between the two. His parents were gone. In truth, he no longer knew how to act around parents.

Charlie dug a handkerchief from his pocket and handed it to Tarah before draping his arm across the back of her chair. He focused on David. "We don't understand what happened. Jonah said Ty was shot by a man who showed up at the office. Was he trying to rob him? Surely he didn't think Ty had any drugs or money lying around at an animal ER."

David didn't know if they knew Coy, so he didn't

know where to start. He went with the easiest explanation. "He stepped in the middle of a domestic assault. This man was attempting to abduct his ex. While the guy was hitting him and dragging him from the building, Tyrone got between them, trying to help."

With his lips pressed in a tight line, Charlie nodded. "That's our Ty. I should've known he was protecting someone. He never could stand to see anyone or anything hurt. Jonah says the guy got away."

David swallowed. Anger and pain made his throat burn. "The police have his name and description. They know where he lives and works. He won't get far."

"What about the other one? The one Ty was trying to help?" Tarah asked. Jonah patted her hand, looking as out of his element as David felt.

David pushed aside the random thought to focus on Tarah's question. "Other than some bruises, he's fine. He did everything he could to help Tyrone until the paramedics arrived. Then he went with the police to give as much information as he could."

"As long as he's safe. That'll matter to Ty when he pulls through this." She sounded so sure—like she knew Tyrone would be fine. David wished he felt anything other than the choking fear of losing Tyrone before they had a chance to build a life. The pain that one thought brought him was unbearable.

"Yes, he's safe," David said absently. Now he just wished someone would tell him the same about Tyrone. As for King, he'd never be safe again as long David lived.

COY HAD COME HOME with a police escort over an hour earlier. From there, he'd gone straight to the stables, where he hadn't stopped pacing since. The horses were restless in their stalls, as if they could smell Coy's agitation. Law knew all this because he'd been sitting out of sight, watching the whole scene the entire time. He waited until Coy turned his back to slip from his hiding spot. Coy looked on the edge of coming completely unglued. Law didn't think he'd take being spied on well.

"How are you holding up?"

Coy startled and spun, looking angry as always. "What do you want from me?"

Law shrugged. "Not a thing. With everything that's going on, I just thought I'd check on you."

Coy shot him an annoyed look, the same way he

always did. It was obvious the boy had zero good feelings toward him. "Why?"

Law rubbed the back of his neck. He was more uncomfortable than he liked. The cut beneath Coy's eye left him feeling hollow—like he wanted to fucking gut someone. The dried blood covering over seventy-five percent of Coy's clothes left him feeling sick. All he could do was deal with the problem in front of him. "Well, I mean, your ex just tried to kill your ex. I'd say that's a full day for anyone."

"Please go away from me," Coy said turning his back on Law.

"I'm not your enemy." The words left Law in a low tone. Part of him hoped Coy didn't hear them.

"The way you treat me says otherwise," Coy muttered, sounding dry and keeping his back turned to Law.

It was true he was hard on Coy. Much harder than he was on anyone else who worked there. But Coy was a better man than he pretended to be, and it frustrated the hell out of Law. He didn't know how to break through Coy's hard shell. Coy was the angriest person he'd ever met. He took a step closer.

Coy spun, looking ready to physically fight him. "What? I'm not on the clock, Law. I don't owe you every aspect of my life and I don't deserve to have you present to witness every horrible fucking thing that happens to me. Walk away."

Law clasped his hands behind his back. "I think you should hit me."

"What?" Coy blinked as if he thought Law had lost his mind. Maybe he had.

"You obviously have a problem with me. So hit me. Like you said, you're off the clock. Get it out of your system while it won't affect your job. It'll probably alleviate that helpless feeling you're drowning in right now."

Coy shook his head, looking tired. His gaze skirted away. He visibly swallowed. "No, thank you. I'm not the typical man. I don't get off on hitting people. It certainly doesn't make me feel better about myself to hurt other people."

Coy's words took Law's breath. In one statement, he said everything Law needed to know. It was no wonder Coy was such a mess. Tyrone was probably the only man who'd never hit Coy. Now Ty was clinging to life for his troubles. When David had brought Coy home, black and blue, Law had seen too much fire in Coy to suspect his injuries were more than a onetime thing. Not to mention, he hadn't gone back to the ass who'd hurt him. That wasn't typical of a beaten down man. Now he saw all the anger for what it was. He'd never be able to unsee it. Coy was a serial victim. He attracted the broken and the weak. Coy tried stepping around him. Law flattened his palm on Coy's chest, stopping him from getting away and ignoring the blood. The light blue eyes that were way too pretty for Law's comfort moved his way and held his gaze. He looked scared—like he expected Law to hurt him. Coy's heart raced beneath Law's palm. Before that moment, it hadn't occurred to Law that Coy lashed out due to fear, not anger.

"I would never hurt you," Law said, keeping his voice steady. He needed Coy to hear the truth in his words. "You're safe here. I would never let *anyone* harm you."

"That's what everyone always says." Coy's words were barely a whisper. "Everyone always lies."

Without thought, Law hauled Coy against him. Coy stood still in his hold, making no attempt to hug him back. He also didn't pull away. Coy was too young to be filled with so much contempt and pain. Law wanted to squeeze it out of him.

"It's okay," Law said, speaking quietly against his ear. "You can close your eyes and pretend you're hugging someone else. My feelings won't be hurt."

A moment passed before Coy's arms encircled Law's waist. His touch was light at first as if he didn't know what to expect. Law held still, trying not to spook him. Obviously deciding Law wouldn't bite, he squeezed Law back. He was so tiny in Law's hold. Fragile.

Law couldn't take it. He had to know. "Who are you holding right now?"

"Me."

Coy's answer was like a punch to the throat. "You're hugging yourself? That's the saddest thing I've ever heard." He didn't mean it the way it sounded. Truly, it broke his heart, but he hadn't meant to say the words aloud. The way Coy tensed, Law knew he'd fucked up.

Coy pushed away before Law could explain. He kept his face averted. "Please stay away from me." The rasp to Coy's voice scared the hell out of Law. He didn't know how to fix anything. Coy didn't give him a chance to figure it out before he walked away. Fuck. He wasn't cut out for this, but someone had to try. Otherwise, he wasn't sure Coy wouldn't turn up dead one day. He cursed under his breath and went after Coy.

"Coy, hold up." Coy didn't slow. Law didn't back down. "If you want, after you get cleaned up, I'll take you to the hospital."

Coy spun so fast, Law stumbled to keep from

barreling him over. "I just want to be left alone. Why is there always some man following me and chasing me? Trying to control me? All I want is—" Coy's shoulders fell. The wind visibly left his sails. His eyes slid closed as his chest expanded on a breath. When he focused on Law again, Law couldn't look away. He needed to know what Coy wanted. Really wanted for himself. There was no way this was it. This place. This life. It didn't fit Coy. Coy was young and beautiful. He deserved more.

"What do you want?" Law asked, keeping his voice low and steady, hoping not to spook Coy.

Coy swallowed hard but didn't look away. "Peace," he said finally, and Law felt it to his soul. "I want to go to sleep without fear. More than anything, I want this voice gone from my head that tells me I don't deserve those things. But the truth is, I'm not good and I don't deserve those things, because look at me," he said with a tired-sounding snort, motioning toward the blood covering his clothes. "This is all my life will ever be. This is all I'll ever bring to the table, and King is right. I'm too stupid for anyone good to want me. That's why I always pick the bad. I'm a plague upon good people. So I'll take my shower and then I'll go. You can breathe a sigh of relief over never having to yell at me again."

As always when dealing with Coy, Law's irritation immediately spiked. "Uh, the hell you say. Is Ty getting shot not enough for you? Will you really not be happy until you're dead?"

Coy's determined expression never wavered. "Better me than anyone else. If I stay, who'll be next? Do you think I want David to get hurt? What about you?"

An ugly snort left Law. "I'm not scared of some pussy who has to hurt people to feel like a man. Let him show up here, because he won't leave here, and you're crazy if you think I'd let you sacrifice yourself for me." Without thought, he reached for Coy. Coy flinched, as if he expected to get hit when Law's hand neared his face. Law moved slower but didn't stop. He gently cupped Coy's check, running his thumb beneath the cut under Coy's eye. He inched closer—like approaching a wild animal. "I promise I'll keep you safe."

A tear slipped from Coy's eye and hit Law's wrist. Law swallowed, hard. Something about Coy's guard coming down punched Law in the throat. "What if Ty dies because of me?"

"Ty won't die. David won't let him, and I won't let anything else happen to you." Law's thumb slipped to Coy's bottom lip. He couldn't stop it from happening. "Just trust me, okay?"

Coy nodded, looking more trusting than Law had seen since he arrived on their doorstep.

"Take your shower. I've got everything else, okay?"

Coy nodded again.

Law let his hand fall away, setting Coy free. As he watched him walk away, Law wondered what the hell he'd just gotten himself into.

NINE

Life screeched to a halt while David sat by Tyrone's bedside. David had never been more thankful for his ability to take control of any situation. Otherwise, Tyrone might have checked himself out of the hospital and gone back to work two days after his surgery. David negotiated a deal with another vet to take on Tyrone's patients. He'd also given all Tyrone's employees six weeks off with pay. The latter might've blown up into a huge argument if Tyrone hadn't worried so much about his staff's welfare. Still, Tyrone repeatedly promised he'd find a way to pay David back. David kept the peace, but there was no way in hell that was happening. It got a little harder every day to keep Tyrone down. He thanked every deity above they were finally home. His everything hurt from sleeping on the pullout in Tyrone's hospital room.

"My poor baby," Tyrone said when David winced for the tenth time as he helped him into bed.

"Joke all you want. You'll be old one day too, and I'll be there to judge you."

Tyrone held his side when his laugh turned into a hiss. He visibly sucked air as he settled into the mountain of pillows David set up for him. David worried at his bottom lip until the pain bled from Tyrone's features. "You're not old," Tyrone argued once he could. "You're sexy and amazing. A little bossy." A small smile hovered on Tyrone's lips. "Perfect."

David rolled his eyes as he stretched out beside Tyrone. He groaned as his bones popped and his muscles relaxed for the first time in two weeks. "Oh my god, Tyrone. Neither of us can ever go back into the hospital for any reason. I can't remember the last time I was this sore, and I wasn't the one who was shot."

"Why do you call me Tyrone?"

David tilted his head at an angle to meet Tyrone's gaze. Tyrone's question seemed an odd change in topic. "What?"

"You always call me Tyrone instead of Ty. I

mean, it's my name, but family and friends call me Ty. You never do."

David rolled and went up on his elbow as he mulled over the question. In truth, it wasn't a conscious effort on his part. He'd been introduced as Tyrone. That was the name that stuck. "Maybe I want to stand out in your life," David said finally, since he didn't have an answer. "Does it bother you?"

Tyrone shook his head. "I was just curious, and you already stand out in my life." Tyrone brushed his fingers through David's hair, massaging his scalp. David's eyes fell closed. Exhaustion and the pleasure of Tyrone's warmth tried pulling him under. "Thank you." Tyrone's quietly spoken words forced his eyes open.

"For?"

Tyrone shrugged. "Never leaving my side. Being here right now. Take your pick from the million wonderful things you've done since we met. I don't feel like life has given me much of a chance to earn you while you've been amazing."

David swallowed a chuckle. He didn't think Tyrone would appreciate it if he laughed at his heartfelt speech. "I'm the one who should be thanking you."

A deep line appeared between Tyrone's eyebrows. "Why?"

"All the same reasons you listed. Plus, you've made me slow down. Do you know how many times I've lounged around in bed in the middle of the day like this?"

"Probably as many times as I have," Tyrone answered with laughter tinging his voice.

David smiled. "Exactly. You've been present for every time I've done it. Through having the flu, breaking bones, and countless other examples, I've never stopped to heal or just linger. Now I know what I missed." He shrugged. "I don't want to be anywhere else right now, and that's something I've never experienced before you. So don't thank me. I'm being selfish." David cleared his throat, dredging up his courage. "In fact, I've been thinking I'd like to be even more selfish. I—" A light knock on the bedroom door drew David up short. He hoped the interruption wasn't a sign he was making a mistake. "Come in."

Coy poked his head inside, looking unsure of his welcome. "Sorry to intrude."

Tyrone waved the boy inside. "It's fine. Come in. We were just taking a break from all the relaxing we did at the hospital." The humor in Tyrone's tone was adorable.

Judging by Coy's smile, he must have thought so as well. His smile slipped away. "I wanted to say that I'm sorry."

According to Law, Coy had been to the hospital, but David hadn't seen him. That meant Tyrone hadn't either. There'd been a small part of David that worried he'd be angry at the first sight of Coy. After all, it had been his trouble that had found them. David realized now he didn't feel that way at all. It wasn't Coy's fault there were bad people in the world. In fact, if not for Coy's quick actions, Tyrone would've died. That was an outcome David couldn't live with.

"None of this is your fault," Tyrone said, as if speaking David's thoughts. "You can't control other people's actions, and if you start thinking you can, you'll be miserable the rest of your life."

David nodded, throwing his support behind Tyrone. "You can only control how you react. Don't let him win by putting this on yourself."

Coy dipped his chin, acknowledging David's words, but his closed expression didn't give David hope that he was really hearing David. "Do either of you need anything? I'm about to go into town."

"You should take Law with you," Tyrone said a little too fast. He visibly tried tempering his reaction. King hadn't been found. It was obvious Tyrone wouldn't feel safe again until that happened.

Something flashed in Coy's eyes. "I have no doubt he's already waiting in the truck."

"Do you mind dropping by my house?" Tyrone asked, obviously satisfied by the fact that Law was tagging along, and turning the conversation away from David's curiosity over Coy's tone. "My mail is probably a foot deep by now."

"No problem. If you need anything else, text me a list, and I'll pick it up while I'm there."

Tyrone rattled off a few items and told Coy where to find his keys. David listened with half an ear, trying not to let his irritation grow. Each word Tyrone spoke was a reminder he didn't truly live here. His spot in David's bed felt temporary. David hated it. His mind churned. The idea of Tyrone moving back home burned in his gut. A black mood scratched at his brain.

Tyrone waved his hand in David's face. "Hello. Are you still with me?"

David blinked. The room came into focus. They were alone. He blinked again. "Sorry. I guess I'm more tired than I realized." He focused on Tyrone. A smile tugged at his lips. Tyrone was settled on a mound of pillows in the most uncomfortable-looking position. Yet he was adorable and looked at home. This was Tyrone's home. Possessiveness filled David's heart to capacity. "I love you."

Tyrone's expression blanked. He blinked, visibly absorbing the words. David didn't think it should be this much of a shock. They'd been together a couple of months now, living together more than half that. It might've been external circumstances that drove them under the same roof, but the result was the same. They were meant to be together. David felt it in his gut. Tyrone's features softened. "I love you too."

A deep breath filled David's lungs. His shoulders relaxed. "Good." He settled down as close to Tyrone's side as he could get without hurting him. Tyrone's hand found his. Their fingers linked. David closed his eyes, letting his body mold to the mattress. A moment passed. The silence stretched out. David felt oddly dissatisfied. "When you're up to it, we should find a place for the rest of your things."

He could feel Tyrone's stare boring into his skin. David kept his eyes shut. He was scared of the rejection he might see in Tyrone's expression. When his pronouncement met with nothing but silence, sleep finally carried David away.

TYRONE LOVED the way David announced his plan to move Tyrone in and then went to sleep. While Tyrone, on the other hand, couldn't stop staring at David. He was so damn beautiful. Inside and out. Everything about David wowed him. Coy had warned him David would move fast. At the time, he'd thought Coy was just being a dick. Maybe he was, but it was still happening. The problem wasn't that David was moving fast. The problem was Tyrone was fine with the pace. There was so much he should be worried about. He should care David was taking over, paying his employees and planning his move. The thing was, he loved David. He hadn't simply returned David's words. Tyrone meant them. His feelings had grown since day one, and then he'd almost died. Nothing could've brought things into perspective more. Life was short. He'd spent too much of his time trying to succeed. Now there was something else he wanted more. Someone.

He hated it hurt each time he moved an inch. Tyrone missed David's touch like crazy. He craved holding him, having David curled against his chest. Each time he thought about David's expression as he'd told Tyrone he loved him, Tyrone fought the urge to wake David. Tyrone had felt the love pouring from David. Seen it in his eyes. He lost the battle against brushing his fingers down David's arm. David snuggled closer but didn't wake.

Their relationship had been ridiculously one-sided with David doing all the work. Tyrone didn't think he deserved David's love. He might be down, but Tyrone wasn't helpless. Snagging his phone, Tyrone shot a quick text off to Jonah. If there was anyone in the world who could help him pull off an over-the-top gesture, it was Jonah's husband John. Tyrone never believed he'd look to John for help, but then again, he'd never thought to love anyone the way he loved David.

TEN

DAVID BLINKED SEVERAL TIMES, TRYING TO adjust to his surroundings. He'd been sleeping at the hospital for so long, he almost didn't recognize his bedroom. A half second after he remembered where he was, David realized the spot next to him was empty. The sleep fog slowing his brain had him staring at the place where Tyrone should be in confusion. He spent so long trying to decide how Tyrone slipped away while injured without disturbing him that he didn't notice the notecard resting on top of the mound of Tyrone's pillows. It was a printed invitation. Happiness had his brain firing on all cylinders as he read.

You are cordially invited to enjoy a night under the stars. Please don your most comfortable sleeping attire and meet your chariot downstairs.

A CHUCKLE RUMBLED from David's chest. He had no idea how Tyrone pulled this off, but he still bounded from the bed. David rushed to the bathroom and ran through his regular morning routine, even though the clock told him it was almost eleven at night. Once sufficiently clean and covered, David headed downstairs. Simone hid a smile when she spotted him. She opened the front door and motioned him outside. A bouquet of roses sat on the hood of the Ranger. Normally, the ATV type vehicle they used to get around the property looked a mess, but now it gleamed in the moonlight. Jonah and Coy sat on the front steps. Both talked animatedly while trying to speak over the top of each other. Coy was smiling in a way David had never seen. He liked the idea of Jonah taking Coy underneath his wing. Jonah was exactly the influence Coy needed in his life. All those thoughts were secondary to his humor over how the pair dressed. They both wore dark tuxedos and top hats. The moment they spotted him, they flew to their feet, wearing matching mischievous smiles.

"Mr. Baker," Jonah called. He motioned toward the Ranger. "Your chariot awaits."

"What's going on?" Even David heard the suspicion in his voice.

Jonah's smile grew. "Allow me to escort you to your destination and you'll find out." His gaze slid down David's body. "A t-shirt and pajama bottoms. Perfect. I'm glad you followed the invitation's instructions." He ascended the steps and reached for David's arm. The moment their arms linked, a wave of adoration washed over David.

After two steps, David found himself pulling Jonah to a stop. He couldn't wait to find out what Tyrone had planned, but he also couldn't let this moment pass. Jonah looked confused as his gaze swung David's way. David patted the hand Jonah had resting in the crook of his arm. "Tyrone's brush with death made me realize a few things. One of those things is that you should always tell people how you feel before it's too late." He took a deep breath, feeling a bit ridiculous, but determined to see this through. "Since the first time we met, I've been fond of you. I've always known I'd never have children. As strange as it might sound, I've thought of you as a son. I know I couldn't be prouder of you if you were mine."

Tears filled Jonah's eyes. He looked away for a moment, blinking. He visibly swallowed before meeting David's stare again. "Thank you for that," Jonah said, sounding hoarse. "I've always wished you were my dad." He kissed David's cheek. "I guess I should call you David from now on."

"I've been trying to get you to do so for years." They both laughed as they headed for the Ranger. Coy stood, holding open the passenger side door for David. He nodded as David slid inside.

Once he was settled, Coy handed the roses to David. "These are for you."

David eyed the flowers as Jonah climbed into the backseat. Coy circled around to the driver's side. He flashed David a smile as he headed down a trail beside the house. "I hope you're ready to be transported into a fantasy."

"This is insane." Even as he made the claim, David couldn't stop smiling. Damn, Tyrone made him happy.

"Most things people do for love are," Coy said, sounding matter-of-fact.

The backs of David's eyes stung. He blinked, trying to alleviate the building pressure. When he'd told Tyrone he loved him, Tyrone had returned the words, but this... David felt loved. Tyrone was hurt and should be in bed. Instead, he'd spent the day doing god knows what, trying to create a special moment for David. No one treated him the way Tyrone did. With as much money as David possessed, everyone assumed he needed nothing. He did. David needed exactly what Tyrone provided.

Coy veered off the trail, cutting between the trees. Tiny white lights hanging from branches led the way to a massive oak. A huge contraption hung from the tree. It looked like a giant swing, but it was a bed with a mosquito net canopy surrounding it. Before the Ranger came to a stop, David spotted John and Law waiting. He didn't see Tyrone. It took every ounce of patience he possessed to stop himself from leaping from the vehicle. Instead, he played along, allowing Jonah to open the door for him.

Jonah's bright smile had David wondering if he looked the same. "When did any of you have time to do this?" He would've thought having such a huge swing installed would take time and professionals.

"You've met John, right?"

At Jonah's question, David snorted. If he'd thought about it, he would've seen John's hand in this. The man Jonah married was the most over-the-top person David had ever met. If David wanted to pull off a huge surprise, John would always be his first call too. He nodded toward John and Law, but he wanted Tyrone.

John met him halfway. His green eyes flashed with devilry, proving how much he enjoyed this. John always took up too much space with his huge shoulders and tall frame. David never thought much about it, but now he blocked the path to Tyrone, and that was the only place David wanted to be. John handed him a bottle of specialty water. "Champagne or wine would be fitting, but Ty can't have anything good yet." He stepped aside and motioned toward the swing. "We've already got Ty settled inside. The swing is temporarily anchored so it won't move or jar him. We plan to keep an extra eye on the property tonight for your safety. Please enjoy a romantic night under the stars."

David's cheeks hurt from smiling. He shook his head at a loss for words. "Thank you."

John patted his shoulder. "No need for that. I'm a sucker for this type of thing."

Jonah sidled up next to John, and they reached for each other at the same time. David's throat swelled. He could remember the exact moment he first looked at them and filled with jealousy, thinking his life would never be like theirs. Now here he was. He pushed aside the netting and spotted Tyrone reclining inside on a mound of pillows.

"Hey, gorgeous."

David bit his bottom lip at Tyrone's greeting. He wondered if his chest would explode from the happiness filling him beyond completion. "Hey, sexy."

"Surprise," Tyrone rasped out, sounding tired.

After setting the flowers and water aside, David climbed in beside him. Concern killed everything else. He touched Tyrone's face, checking for any sign of fever. Even though it had been a couple of weeks, David still hadn't shaken the fear of losing Tyrone. Since the moment he learned they were coming home, terror over every little complication that could arise choked him. "Are you okay? You shouldn't have done all this. You're supposed to be resting."

Tyrone clasped David's hand between his, stopping him from fussing. "It's okay, baby. I'm fine. You're not getting rid of me that easily. I'm just tired because I'm still healing. Everyone else did all this for me. I relaxed and gave suggestions." He shifted, making room in his pillow mound. "Cuddle with me."

David's shoulders relaxed. Worry still owned

him, but he gave Tyrone his wish and cuddled against his side. He did his best not to touch Tyrone's stomach. "This was very sweet."

Tyrone kissed his forehead. "When I'm better, this can be our spot. A bed under the stars whenever we want. It's supposed to swing, but they had to anchor it for now."

David stared up at the night sky. It looked twice as beautiful, sharing it with Tyrone. "This is amazing." Another thought hit David. He realized, a little slower than he should have, the significance of the gift. "Since you've claimed a tree for us, does that mean you're moving in for good?"

A soft chuckle filled the air. "You sort of demanded it of me earlier and then fell asleep."

Heat flooded David's cheeks. He cleared his throat. "Yeah, I guess I can be a little controlling. If you don't want to live here, I won't be angry. I get that you're a grown man and should get to decide."

Tyrone toyed with David's fingers before bringing them to his lips. He trailed kisses along David's hand, causing goosebumps to rise on his skin. "Don't take it back now," Tyrone whispered. "I just got used to the idea that you're mine every night from here on out. There'll never be another night I don't get to hold you. I'll get to kiss you and tell you I love you." David soaked up every word, fighting the burning behind his eyes. Tyrone kept talking, painting an image of a life together that David wanted more than he could express. "I also have a bit of news. You know how John has a hell of a sales pitch."

David nodded, squishing his cheek against Tyrone's chest. He didn't trust his voice.

"Well," Tyrone said, taking a deep breath. "I let him sell me on an idea for a Green's Puppy Fuel. In exchange for helping him design a specialty dog food formula, using his company's ingredients, and selling the products at my office, he plans to pay me enough that I can afford to bring in some help, so I don't have to work as much or be there as often. That way, I can dedicate more time to this."

By the end of Tyrone's speech, David had his lips pressed together, trying not to shout his excitement. Despite knowing Tyrone was busy going into their relationship, David couldn't deny he wanted more of Tyrone's time than he currently got. "Out of all the wonderful things you've done today, I think that one is the best." David stared at the sky. A smile touched his lips. "This is pretty damn awesome too. I can see us spending our nights here whenever the mood strikes." His smile fell. "Damn, I don't want to spend the rest of our lives with our friends scouring the property, looking for threats. I want you to feel safe again."

Tyrone's lips skimmed the shell of David's ear. His warm breath made David's goosebumps worse. "You don't have to worry about anything, baby. Whether they ever catch King or if he turns up dead in an alley in Mexico, no one can take me from you. I refuse to let some piece of shit bully have the power to make me live in fear."

"Hey, guys." They froze at the quietly spoken words right outside their haven. "I don't want to bother you."

David realized it was Coy. With the bright stars and full moon, he could somewhat make out the guy's features through the mosquito netting. "Hey, Coy. You're not bothering us. Is everything okay?"

Coy flipped open the flap on the netting and poked his head inside. "I don't want to burst in on your date. I just thought you'd like to know that the detective in charge of our case called. He said a body washed up on Las Maritos beach and they've identified the person as King, so I guess no more looking over our shoulders." Coy spun his cellphone between his fingers, looking nervous. David was torn. He was glad King was dead. On the other hand, no matter how horrible of a human King was, there'd been a time when he'd mattered to Coy. David couldn't imagine the mixed emotions that must be roiling inside Coy.

"Are you okay?" Tyrone asked, beating David to the punch and proving—as always—their thoughts matched.

A sad smile touched Coy's lips. "I don't know."

David and Tyrone exchanged a glance. As one, they scooted over, making room for Coy. "Get in here."

At David's demand, Coy shook his head. "You two need some time to yourselves. I just hoped to give you one less thing to worry about."

"He wasn't asking," Tyrone said, making David proud.

Coy hesitated another few seconds before gingerly climbing inside with them. "Will this thing hold all of us?" Coy asked as he settled in next to David.

Tyrone urged David closer, stroking his arm. "Yeah. The company John found to install it, this is all they do. They know how to choose the perfect tree and anchor everything, so it'll last for years. There's no way I would've risked ripping open my stitches, so my insides fall out, by choosing some shoddy equipment. Don't change the subject, though. It's okay for you to feel torn over this."

Silence stretched between them for several long minutes before Coy finally responded. "The detective says it looks like King died from a self-inflicted gunshot wound. I feel like this was the final fuck you to me from King, you know? Like every bad thing he did wasn't enough. He also had to leave me feeling guilty for hoping he'd turn up dead. It's just... odd, knowing someone I once... never mind. I really don't know how to feel. Well," Coy quickly tacked on, "I do know one thing. Don't fuck with someone Jonah loves."

A bark of surprised laughter escaped David. "What's that supposed to mean?"

David felt more than saw Coy shrug. "When I first met Jonah, he said he knew a guy who could break King's kneecaps. Obviously, I thought he was joking. Then I met Jonah's husband, and I realized I'd seen him before—back when I worked nights at the casino inside Luna Hotel. He's friends with the owner." Coy shrugged again—like that was the end of the story.

When he didn't say anything else, David's curiosity got the best of him. "What does that have to do with anything? Green's Fighter Fuel sponsors a lot of MMA fighters. Luna is where the fights are held. There's nothing strange about that."

The moonlight glimmered off Coy's eyes, making them appear to sparkle in the dark. "Luna hotel is owned by the Russian mafia," Coy said, as if it was common knowledge.

The full implications of Coy's words sank in. David's first reaction was to laugh away the idea that something so sinister could've been set in motion by someone as sweet as Jonah. The laughter died in his throat before it came to light. David honestly couldn't see Jonah doing such a thing, but John... If Jonah was upset enough over Tyrone, David wasn't sure there was any length that was too far for John when it came to Jonah's happiness. Not to mention if John thought there was any chance Jonah might be in danger while volunteering for Tyrone... He shook his head. It was ridiculous to think anyone would possibly make that connection. John and Jonah were both too nice. David wouldn't consider it. "Everyone is safe. That's what matters. You can start a new life."

"Which I hope doesn't include leaving us," Tyrone said, making David want to happy dance. Tyrone was already speaking like this place was their home and they were a team. Damn, he couldn't wait for Tyrone to be back on his feet, so David could sweep him off them.

"I'm not ready to leave here, if that's okay with the two of you. It's just, I'm not ready," Coy repeated, sounding as if he worried they'd judge him.

"We want you here," David said, having Tyrone's back.

Coy gave him a sharp nod. "I'm really going to leave the two of you alone now. It's nice of you to try to comfort me, but really, I'm used to dealing on my own. I prefer it that way."

David blew out a sigh. "Okay, but you know where we are should you change your mind."

Coy flashed him a sweet smile before slipping away. David watched him go while enjoying the warmth of being in Tyrone's arms. Tyrone kissed the shell of his ear, moving lower and lightly nibbling his earlobe. David drew a slow breath in through his nose. It would likely be weeks before they could make love again. Tyrone was too much of a temptation.

"Hopefully, he'll be okay," Tyrone breathed against his ear. He kissed the spot beneath it, making David's eyes fall closed. "Roll this way." At Tyrone's quietly spoken demand, David's eyes flew open. He met Tyrone's stare. There was no mistaking the heat etching Tyrone's features.

"Um. My willpower's not that strong."

Tyrone didn't back down. "Roll this way."

David rolled, facing Tyrone. "You'd better not tear anything."

A low, evil-sounding chuckle rumbled from the back of Tyrone's throat, making David go hard. Tyrone's fingers found the knot in David's pants. He worked it loose. "Just because I'm incapacitated, that doesn't mean I'm incapable of pleasing you."

David's mouth went dry. "Promise me you won't hurt yourself." Damn, a hard dick made him stupid.

"Kiss me," Tyrone demanded instead.

David moved higher and pressed his lips to Tyrone's. Tyrone's lips immediately parted, giving David the freedom to toy with Tyrone's tongue. The lightest of touches skimmed his cock. David sucked in a ragged breath. Tyrone skimmed the tips of his fingers down David's erection again. David's breathing deepened. There was no pumping or quick motions that could hurt Tyrone. Instead, Tyrone lightly stroked his fingertips up and down David's dick, barely teasing him. Yet David's entire being focused on the sensation. His hips rolled, trying to get closer. Tyrone didn't let up. He traced

David's crown and then lightly stroked him to his root before starting over again. It was maddening. David found himself kissing Tyrone deeper while savoring the slow pleasure of Tyrone's touch. Soft moans rose in his throat, leaving him in a whimper. Tyrone's breathing turned labored. David leaned away, worried.

"I didn't say you could stop kissing me," Tyrone growled, sounding desperate. David reclaimed his lips because he couldn't deny Tyrone anything. Every muscle in David's body tensed to the point he feared he'd tear something. The pressure beating at his crown begged for release. David refused to help things along. He loved Tyrone's slow, torturous pleasuring. Everything narrowed to a pinpoint. David covered his cock with his t-shirt, catching his cum with the material as his orgasm hit. He wouldn't risk soaking Tyrone's bandages in any way. Tyrone's breath hitched against David's tongue, as if David's pleasure was his.

"Goddamn, I love you," Tyrone rasped, sounding desperate.

"I love you too," David gasped. He pressed his forehead to Tyrone's chest and rode out every wave. He hated things being one-sided like this, but he'd make it up to Tyrone. In fact, he'd make every day of

Tyrone's life so fucking perfect, there wouldn't be a single moment Tyrone didn't recognize the truth. He was the love of David's life. His one true obsession. There was no length he wouldn't go for Tyrone, even if it meant calling in a favor from an old friend who owned a casino near Las Maritos beach. There was no length too far at all.

Keep an eye out for the next Sugar Daddies, *Sugar Enemy*.

Please consider leaving a review at the retailer where this book was purchased. Reviews really help with a book's visibility, which ensures I can continue writing. Thank you, Charity.

ABOUT THE AUTHOR

Charity Parkerson is an award winning and multi-published author with several companies. Born with no filter from her brain to her mouth, she decided to take this odd quirk and insert it in her characters.

*Eight-time Readers' Favorite Award Winner

    *2015 Passionate Plume Award Finalist

    *2013 Reviewers' Choice Award Winner

    *2012 ARRA Finalist for Favorite Paranormal Romance

    *Five-time winner of The Mistress of the Darkpath

Connect with her online:

--Join my street team: facebook.com/TeamCharityParkerson

    --Sign up for my newsletter: http://bit.ly/CharityNews

--Website: charityparkerson.com

--Facebook:

facebook.com/authorCharityParkerson

facebook.com/TheMenofSin

--Twitter: twitter.com/CharityParkerso